THE N
BEEN W

BY
MEREDITH WEBBER

MILLS & BOON®
Pure reading pleasure

All the characters in this book have no existence outside the imagination of the author, and have no relation whatsoever to anyone bearing the same name or names. They are not even distantly inspired by any individual known or unknown to the author, and all the incidents are pure invention.

All Rights Reserved. whole or in part no any the ment with Harle ation or any p ny form or by copying, record herwise, witho

This b y way of trade irculated witho nding or cover similar condi bsequent purch

® and TM are trademarks owned and used by the trademark owner and/or its licensee. Trademarks marked with ® are registered with the United Kingdom Patent Office and/or the Office for Harmonisation in the Internal Market and in other countries.

First published in Great Britain 2007
Harlequin Mills & Boon Limited,
Eton House, 18-24 Paradise Road, Richmond, Surrey TW9 1SR

© Meredith Webber 2007

ISBN: 978 0 263 85267 7

Set in Times Roman 10½ on 12 pt
03-1007-45227

Printed and bound in Spain
by Litografia Rosés, S.A., Barcelona

Meredith Webber says of herself, 'Some years ago, I read an article which suggested that Mills & Boon were looking for new medical authors. I had one of those "I can do that" moments, and gave it a try. What began as a challenge has become an obsession, though I do temper the "butt on seat" career of writing with dirty but healthy outdoor pursuits, fossicking through the Australian Outback in search of gold or opals. Having had some success in all of these endeavours, I now consider I've found the perfect lifestyle.'

Recent titles by the same author:

HIS RUNAWAY NURSE
THE SPANISH DOCTOR'S CONVENIENT BRIDE
A FATHER BY CHRISTMAS
BRIDE AT BAY HOSPITAL
THE DOCTOR'S MARRIAGE WISH*

*Crocodile Creek

Dear Reader

Writing is such a solitary pursuit that to be involved in a series with other people is really special. To be involved in a series with three good friends—Marion Lennox, Lilian Darcy and Alison Roberts—is extraordinarily special. More than that, it's tremendous fun. Although we live far apart, three of us in different states in Australia and Alison in New Zealand, we do manage to get together most years at the Australian Romance Writers' Conference.

It was at one of these conferences about four years ago that the idea for the *Crocodile Creek* series was born. The four of us spent more time in various hotel bedrooms plotting out our masterpiece than we did listening to conference speakers. Then we had to sell the idea to our editors, which took a little time and quite a lot of work on their part and on ours, but in the end we got the go-ahead and suddenly Crocodile Creek became as real to us as our home suburbs, and the people who worked in the hospital and Air Rescue Service became our friends.

I was very fond of Harry, the policeman, so was delighted when I could match him up with Grace in this book. Grace's sunny nature and helpful personality make her the ideal woman for Harry, but she fears she is unlovable and he just flat-out fears love. But as a cyclone whirls above their heads, things change.

And now? Well, while we might have sorted out the love-lives of some of our friends in this second series, several new people have appeared who might also need some loving. I hope so, as being involved in the series has been special—almost as special as being in love.

Meredith Webber

PROLOGUE

As A cyclone hovered off the coast of North Queensland, threatening destruction to any town in its path, several hundred miles away a small boy sneaked on board a bus. Terrified that his father, who was arguing with the bus driver, would discover the dog he'd threatened to drown, Max ducked between the two men and climbed the steps into the warm, fusty, dimly lit interior of the big vehicle. Mum would sort everything out when he got to Crocodile Creek—the fare, the dog, everything.

Mum would like a dog.

'Don't call her Mum—she's your flippin' sister! Or half-sister, if you really want to know.'

Echoes of his father's angry rant rang through Max's head, but Georgie hadn't ever minded him calling her Mum, and it stopped kids at school teasing him.

The kids that had mums, that was.

Mum would love Scruffy.

He shifted the backpack off his shoulder and hugged it to his chest, comforted by the squirming of the pup inside it, checking out the passengers as he made his way up the aisle. He'd been shunted back and forth across Queensland often enough to be able to pick out who was who among his fellow travellers.

The bus was nearly full and all the usual ones were there. A group of backpackers chattering away in a foreign language, a fat woman in the seat behind them—bet she'd been to visit her grandkids—bloke on the other side of the aisle—he'd be late back on the bus at all the rest stops—an old couple who looked like they'd been on the bus for all of their lives, and a tired, sad-looking woman with a little boy.

Max slipped into the seat behind them. He'd never told Mum and certainly wouldn't bother telling Dad, but scary things could happen on a bus, and he'd worked out it's always best to stick with someone with a kid, or to sit near a youngish couple, so he looked like part of a family.

Though with Scruffy to protect him…

He slid across the seat to the window, looking for his father, wondering if the argument was over—if his father had actually paid to get rid of him this time.

Wanting to wave goodbye.

The footpath was deserted, the bus driver now talking to someone in the doorway of the travel office. Twisting his head against the glass, Max could just make out a shambling figure moving through a pool of lamplight well behind the bus—walking away from it.

So much for waving goodbye.

'It doesn't matter!' Max told himself fiercely, scrunching up his eyes and blinking hard, turning his attention to the zip on his backpack before thrusting his hand inside, feeling Scruffy's rough hair, a warm tongue licking his fingers. 'It doesn't matter!'

But when you're only seven, it did matter…

CHAPTER ONE

MIDNIGHT, and Grace O'Riordan lay on one of the examination couches in the emergency department of the Crocodile Creek Hospital and stared at an amoeba-shaped stain on the ceiling as she contemplated clothes, love and the meaning of life.

In truth, the meaning of life wasn't overtaxing her brain cells right now, and she'd assured herself, for the forty-hundredth time, that the dress she'd bought for the wedding wasn't too over the top, which left love.

Love, as in unrequited.

One-sided.

Heavens to Betsy, as if she hadn't had enough one-sided love in her life.

Perhaps loving without being loved back made her unlovable. In the same way old furniture, polished often, developed a rich deep shiny patina, so loved people shone and attracted more love.

What *was* this? Sensible, practical, Grace O'Riordan indulging in wild flights of fancy? She'd be better off napping.

Although she was on duty, the A and E dept—in fact,

the entire hospital—after a particularly hectic afternoon and early evening, was quiet. Quiet enough for her to have a sleep, which, given the frantic few days she'd just spent checking on cyclone preparations, she needed.

But she needed love, too, and was practical—there was that word again—enough to know that she had to get over her present love—the unrequited one—and start looking to the future. Start looking for someone who might love her back, someone who also wanted love and the things that went with it, like marriage and a family. Especially a family. She had been family-less for quite long enough...

This coming week would provide the perfect opportunity to begin the search, with people flying in from all over the globe for the weddings of Mike and Emily tomorrow and, a week later, Gina and Cal. Surely somewhere, among all the unattached male wedding guests, there'd be someone interested in a smallish, slightly plump, sometimes pretty, Irish-Australian nurse.

She pressed her hand against her heart, sure she could feel pain just thinking about loving someone other than Harry.

But she'd got over love before, she could do it again.

'Move on, Grace!' she told herself, in her sternest voice.

'Isn't anyone on duty in this place?' a loud voice demanded.

Harry's voice.

Grace slid off the table, pulled her uniform shirt straight, wondered, briefly, whether her short curls looked like a flattened bird's nest after lying down, and exited the room to greet the man she was trying to get over.

'If you'd come in through the emergency door, a bell would have rung and I'd have known you were here,' she greeted him, none too warmly. Then she saw the blood.

'Holy cow, Harry Blake, what have you done to yourself this time?'

She grabbed a clean towel from a pile on a trolley and hurried towards the chair where he'd collapsed, one bloody leg thrust out in front of him.

Wrapping the towel tightly around the wound to stem at least some of the bleeding, she looked up into his face. Boy, was it ever hard to get over love when her heart danced jigs every time she saw him.

Irish jigs.

She looked at his face again—as a nurse this time. It was grey with tiredness but not, as far as she could tell, pale from blood loss.

'Can you make it into an examination cubicle or will I ring for help?' she asked, knowing full well he was so stubborn he'd refuse help even if she called for it. But when he stood he wobbled slightly, so she tucked her shoulder into his armpit to take some of his weight, and with her arm around his back for added support she led him into the room.

He sat down on the couch she'd occupied only minutes earlier, then, as she pushed at his chest and lifted his legs, he lay down.

'What happened?' she asked, as she unwrapped the towel enough to know there was no arterial bleeding on his leg, then wrapped it up again so she could check his vital signs before she examined the wound.

'Carelessness,' he muttered at her. He closed his eyes, which made her wonder if his blood loss was more serious than she'd supposed. But his pulse was strong, his blood pressure excellent and his breathing steady. Just to be sure, she slid an oxygen saturation meter onto one of his fingers, and turned on the monitor.

'What kind of carelessness?' she asked as she once again unwrapped the towel and saw the torn, blood-stained trouser leg and the badly lacerated skin beneath the shredded fabric.

'Chainsaw! Does that stain on the ceiling look like a penguin to you?'

'No, it looks like an amoeba, which is to say a formless blob.' She was using scissors to cut away his trousers, so she could see the wound. Blood had run into his sock, making it hard to tell if the damage went down that far. Taking care not to brush against his wound, she took hold of his boot to ease it off.

'You can't do that,' he said, sitting up so quickly his shoulder brushed against her and his face was kissing close.

Kissing Harry? As if!

'Can't take your boot off?' she asked. 'Is there some regulation about not being a policeman if you're not wearing both boots?'

He turned towards her, a frown pleating his black eyebrows, his grey eyes perplexed. 'Of course not. You just wouldn't get it off.' He tugged and twisted at the same time and the elastic-sided boot slid off. 'I'll get the sock, too,' he added, pulling off the bloodstained wreck, but not before Grace had noticed the hole at the top of the big toe.

In a dream where Harry loved her back, she'd have mended that hole—she'd like doing things like that— the little caring things that said *I love you* without the words.

'Lie back,' she said, dream and reality coming too close for comfort with him sitting there. 'I'll flush this mess and see what's what.'

She pulled on clean gloves and set a bag of saline on a drip stand. She'd need tubing, a three-way tap, syringe and a nineteen-gauge needle to drip the liquid onto the wound while she probed for foreign particles.

Packing waterproof-backed absorbent pads beneath his leg, she started the saline dripping onto the wound, a nasty contusion running eight inches in length, starting on the tibia just below the knee and swerving off into his calf.

'The skin's so chewed up it's not viable enough to stitch,' she told him, probing a few pieces of what looked like mangled treetrunk, or possibly mangled trouser fabric, from the deepest part. Organic matter and clay were among the most likely things to cause infection in tissue injury. 'Ideally it should be left open, but I guess you're not willing to stay home and rest it for the next few days.'

'You *are* joking!' Harry said. 'I need it patched up now, and maybe in three days' time, when we know for sure Cyclone Willie has departed, I can rest it.'

'Harry, it's a mess. I'll dress it as best I can but if you don't look after it and come in to have it dressed every day, you're going to end up with ulceration and needing a skin graft on it.'

She left the saline dripping on the wound while she

found the dressings she'd need and some antibiotic cream which she would spread beneath the non-adhesive dressing once she had all visible debris removed from it.

Harry watched her work, right up until she starting snipping away torn tatters of skin, when he turned his attention back to the penguin on the ceiling.

'Would you like me to give you a local anaesthetic while I do this? It could hurt.'

'It *is* hurting,' he said, gritting his teeth as a particularly stubborn piece of skin or grit defied Grace's efforts to be gentle. 'But, no, no needles. Just talk to me. And before you do, have another look—maybe the stain looks like the little engine on a cane train.'

Grace glanced towards the ceiling but shook her head as she turned back towards him.

'Since when do a penguin and a cane train engine share similarities in looks?'

'It's a shape thing,' he said, grabbing at her hand and drawing the shape on the back of it. 'Penguin, blob, train engine, see?'

'Not even vaguely,' she told him, rescuing her hand from his grasp then changing her gloves again before she continued with her job. 'And I can see right through you, Harry Blake. You're babbling on about penguins and cane trains to keep me from going back to the question you avoided earlier.'

She stopped talking while she spread cream across his leg. He didn't feel much like talking either.

Grace sealed the wound with a broad, long dressing, and bandaged over it with crêpe bandages, then pulled a long sleeve over the lot, giving it as much security and padding as she could because she knew he'd be putting himself in situations where he could bump it.

'That should give it some protection from physical damage, although, with the cyclone coming, who knows what you'll be called on to do? Just make sure you come in to have it checked and re-dressed every day.'

'You on duty tomorrow?'

Grace smiled sadly to herself. Would that he was asking because he was interested!

'You already know the answer to that one. I finish night duty in the morning and have three days off so I can cope with the wedding and the cyclone preparations without letting any one down here at the hospital.'

Harry sat up and swung his legs over the side of the bed, ready to leave.

'Not so fast,' she warned him. 'I need to check your tetanus status and give you some antibiotics just in case there's some infection already in there.'

She paused and her wide blue eyes met his.

'*And* you're not leaving here until you tell me how you did it.'

Harry studied her as he debated whether to tell her. Tousled curls, freckled nose—Grace, everyone's friend.

His friend, too. A friendship formed when he'd been in need of a friend in the months after Nikki's death. True, he'd had friends, good friends, among the townspeople and the hospital staff, but all the locals had known Nikki since she'd been a child while the hospital staff had all drawn close to her as they'd nursed her through the last weeks of her life.

And though these friends had all stood by him and

had wanted to offer support, he'd avoided them, not wanting sympathy, needing to be left alone to sort out the morass of conflicting emotions warring within him.

Grace had arrived after Nikki's death, so there was no connection, no history, just a bright, bubbly, capable young woman who was willing to listen if he wanted to talk, to talk if he needed conversation, or just to share the silence when he didn't want to be alone.

A true friend…

'I'm waiting!'

She had her hands on her hips and a no-nonsense look on her face, but though she was trying to look serious a smile lurked in her blue eyes.

A smile nearly always lurked in Grace's eyes…

The thought startled him to the extent that confession seemed easier than considering what, if anything, noticing Grace's smiling eyes might mean.

'I hit my leg with the blade of a chainsaw.'

'And *what* were you doing, wielding a chainsaw, may I ask?'

'A tree had come down, out along the Wygera road, but part of the trunk must have been dead because the saw bounced off it when it hit it.' He waved his hand towards his now securely bandaged leg. 'One wounded leg.'

'That wasn't my question and you know it, Harry. It's one o'clock in the morning. You're a policeman, not a rescue worker. The fire service, the electricity workers and, or when requested, the SES crews clear roads. It's what they're trained to do. The SES manual has pages and pages on safe working with chainsaws.'

'I've been using chainsaws all my life,' Harry

retorted, uncomfortably aware this conversation might not be about chainsaws but uncertain what it was about.

'That's not the point,' Grace snapped. 'What if the accident had been worse? What if you'd taken your leg off? Then who's in charge here? Who's left to co-ordinate services to a town that could be struck by one of the worst cyclones in history within the next twenty-four hours?'

'Give over, Grace,' he said, standing up on his good leg and carefully putting weight on the injured one to see how bad it felt.

Very bad. Bad enough to make him feel queasy.

'No, I won't give over.' No smile in the blue eyes now. In fact, she was glaring at him. 'This is just typical of you, Harry Blake. Typical of the stupid risks you take. You mightn't care what happens to you, but you've got family and friends who do. There are people out there who'd be deeply hurt if you were killed or badly injured, but do you think about them when you pull on your superhero cape and go rushing blindly into danger? No, you don't! You don't think of anyone but yourself, and that's not noble or self-sacrificing or even brave—it's just plain selfishness, Harry.'

Harry heard her out, growing more annoyed every second. He'd had a shocking day, he was tired, his leg hurt and to accuse him of selfishness, well, that was just the last straw.

'And just what makes you think you have the right to sit in judgement on me?' he demanded, taking a careful stride towards the cubicle curtain so he could escape any further conversation. 'What makes you think you know me well enough to call me selfish, or to question my motives in helping people? You're not my mother or my wife, Grace, so butt out!'

He heard her gasp as he headed out of the cubicle, across the deserted A and E waiting room and out of the hospital, limping not entirely because of his leg but because he was only wearing one boot. The other he'd stupidly left behind, and that made him even angrier than Grace's accusation. He looked up at the cloud-massed sky and wanted to yell his frustration to the wind.

Perhaps it was just as well there was no one around, although if he'd happened on someone he knew he could have asked that person to go back in and retrieve the boot for him. The hospital was quieter than he'd ever seen it, with no one coming or going from the car park.

He was contemplating radioing the constable on duty to come over and collect it for him when he heard the footsteps behind him.

Grace!

Coming to apologise?

'Here's your boot, and some antibiotics, directions on when to take them on the packet. And in answer to your question about rights, I thought, for some obviously foolish reason, I had the right of a friend.'

And with that she spun on her heel and walked briskly back into the hospital.

Wonderful! Now Grace had joined the throng of people he'd somehow managed to upset, simply because they refused to let him get on with his life his way.

Alone! With no emotional involvement with anyone or anything.

Except Sport, the three-legged blue heeler cattle dog he'd rescued from the dump one day.

And his parents—he liked his parents. And they'd known him well enough to back off when Nikki had died...

He climbed into his vehicle and slumped back against the seat. Was the day over? Please, God, it might be. On top of all the damage and power disruptions caused by the gale-force winds stirred up by Cyclone Willie, he'd had to handle traffic chaos at the fishing competition, an assault on Georgie Turner, the local ob-stetrician, Sophia Poulos, mother of the groom at the next day's wedding, phoning every fifteen minutes to ask about the cyclone as if he was personally respon-sible for its course, and to top it all off, he'd had to visit Georgie again.

She was still shaken from the assault by a patient's relative earlier that day, and nursing a hairline fracture to her cheekbone. Now Harry had to tell her there was a summons out for her stepfather's arrest—her stepfa-ther who currently had custody of her little brother Max.

Did Georgie know where he was?

She hadn't known where the pair were, and he'd hated himself for asking because now she'd be even more worried about Max, whom she'd loved and cared for since he'd been a baby, bringing him up herself—except for the times when the worthless scoundrel who'd fathered him swooped in and took him away, no doubt to provide a prop in some nefarious purpose.

Max was such a great kid, growing up around the hospital, loved and watched out for by everyone in the close-knit community.

So Harry had been driving away from the doctors' house, seething with frustration that he couldn't offer anything to help the white-faced, injured woman, when the call had come in about the tree coming down to block the Wygera road. His chainsaw had already been in the vehicle so he'd decided to take out some of his anger and frustration on a tree.

None of which was any excuse for being rude to Grace...

Not wanting to think about Harry or the crushing words he'd used, Grace retreated to cubicle one once again and climbed back onto the examination couch. She stared at the stain on the ceiling, trying to see a penguin or a cane train engine but seeing only an amoeba.

Was it because she lacked imagination?

Not that she couldn't see the penguin but that she couldn't let Harry alone to get on with his life his own way.

Did her lack of imagination mean she couldn't understand his grieving process?

Hurt enveloped her—that Harry could say what he had. And while she knew she should have welcomed his angry comment because now she knew for sure she had to move on, such rational reasoning didn't make the pain any less.

She studied the stain.

'Is this place totally deserted?'

Another male voice, this one deep and slightly husky. Grace sprang off the couch and was about to emerge from the treatment cubicle when the curtain opened.

Luke Bresciano, hunky, dark amber-eyed, black-haired, Italian-Australian orthopod, stood there, smiling at her.

'I always napped on examination couches when I was on duty in the ER, and for some reason it's always treatment room one,' he teased.

He had a lovely smile but it didn't reach his eyes—a tortured soul, Dr B. And although, this being Crocodile Creek, stories about his past abounded—a woman who'd left him, a child—no one really knew any more about him than they had the day he'd arrived. Age, marital status and qualifications.

'You're here late. Do you have a patient coming in?' Grace asked, being practical and professional while wondering if she remembered how to flirt and if there was any point in trying a little flirtation on Luke. Although was there any point in swapping one tortured soul for another?

'I find sleep comes when it wants to and it wasn't coming so I drove up to see a patient I'd admitted earlier. I looked in on Susie while I was here—'

'Susie? Our physio Susie? In hospital? But she can't be.' Grace was stumbling over her disbelief. 'She's Emily's bridesmaid tomorrow. Mrs Poulos will have a cow!'

Luke offered a kindly smile—much like the one Grace usually offered drunks or people coming out of anaesthetic who were totally confused.

'You obviously haven't heard the latest. Susie had a fall and sprained her ankle earlier today—or is it yesterday now? But the bridesmaid thing's been sorted out. Her twin sister Hannah is here—they're identical twins—and she's going to do bridesmaid duties so the photos won't—'

'Be totally spoilt by Susie's crutches,' Grace finished for him, shaking her head in bemusement that such a wonderful solution—from Mrs P.'s point of view—had been found. Grace was quite sure Emily wouldn't have minded in the least.

Nodding agreement to her ending of the story, Luke finished, 'Exactly! So after visiting Susie, who was sound asleep anyway, I was taking a short cut out through here when I realised how empty it seemed.'

He smiled at Grace but although it was a very charming smile, it did nothing to her heart. She'd really have to work on it if she wanted to move on from Harry. 'I thought I'd better check we did have someone on duty.'

'Yes, that's me. I can't believe how quiet it is. All I heard from the day staff was how busy they'd been and I was busy earlier but now…'

She waved her arms around to indicate the emptiness.

'Then I'll let you get back to sleep,' Luke said.

He turned to depart and she remembered the stain.

'Before you go, would you mind having a look at this stain?'

The words were out before she realised just how truly weird her request was, but Luke was looking enquiringly at her, so she pointed at the stain on the ceiling.

'Roof leaking? I'm not surprised given the rain we've been having, but Maintenance probably knows more about leaking roofs than I do. In fact, they'd have to.' Another charming smile. 'I know zilch.'

'It's not a leak. It's an old stain but I'd really like to know what you think about the shape. You have to lie down on the couch to see it properly. Would you mind checking it out and telling me what it looks like to you?'

'Ink-blot test, Grace?' Luke teased, but he lay obediently on the couch and turned his attention to the stain.

'It looks a bit like a penguin to me,' Luke said, and Grace was sorry she'd asked.

She walked out to the door with Luke, said goodbye, then returned to the cubicle.

It *must* be lack of imagination that she couldn't see it. She focussed on the stain, desperate to see the penguin and prove her imaginative abilities.

Hadn't she just imagined herself darning Harry's socks?

The stain remained a stain—amoeba-like in its lack of form. She clambered off the couch, chastising herself for behaving so pathetically.

For heaven's sake, Grace, get over it!

Get over Harry and get on with your life.

She stood and stared at the stain, trying for a cane train engine this time…

Trying not to think about Harry…

Failing…

It had come as a tumultuous shock to Grace, the realisation that she was love with Harry. She, who'd vowed never to risk one-sided love again, had fallen into the trap once more. She'd fallen in love with a man who'd been there and done that as far as love and marriage were concerned.

A man who had no intention of changing his single status.

They'd been at a State Emergency Service meeting, and had stayed behind, as they nearly always did, to chat. Grace was team leader of the Crocodile Creek SES and Harry, as the head of the local police force, was the co-ordinator for all rescue and emergency services in the area.

Harry had suggested coffee, as he nearly always did after their fortnightly meetings. Nothing noteworthy there—coffee was coffee and all Grace's defences had been securely in place. They'd locked the SES building and walked the short distance down the road to the Black Cockatoo, which, although a pub, also served the best coffee in the small community of Crocodile Creek.

The bar had been crowded, a group of young people celebrating someone's birthday, making a lot of noise and probably drinking a little too much, but Harry Blake, while he'd keep an eye on them, wasn't the kind of policeman who'd spoil anyone's innocent fun.

So he'd steered Grace around the corner where the bar angled, leaving a small, dimly lit area free from noise or intrusion.

The corner of the bar had been dark, but not too dark for her to see Harry's grey eyes glinting with a reflection of the smile on his mobile lips and Harry's black hair flopping forward on his forehead, so endearingly her fingers had ached to push it back.

'Quieter here,' he said, pulling out a barstool and taking Grace's elbow as she clambered onto it. Then he smiled—nothing more. Just a normal, Harry Blake kind of smile, the kind he offered to men, women, kids and

dogs a million times a day. But the feeble defences
Grace O'Riordan had built around her heart collapsed
in the warmth of that smile, and while palpitations
rattled her chest, and her brain tut-tutted helplessly,
Grace realised she'd gone and done it again.

Fallen in love.

With Harry, of all people...

Harry, who was her friend...

CHAPTER TWO

GRACE fidgeted with the ribbon in her hair. It was too much—she knew it was too much. Yet the woman in the mirror looked really pretty, the ribbon somehow enhancing her looks.

She took a deep breath, knowing it wasn't the ribbon worrying her but Harry, who was about to pick them all up to drive them to the wedding.

The hurtful words he'd uttered very early that morning—*you're not my mother or my wife*—still echoed in her head, made worse by the knowledge that what he'd said was true. She *didn't* have the right to be telling Harry what to do!

It was a good thing it had happened, she reminded herself. She had to get past this love she felt for him. She'd had enough one-sided love in her life, starting in her childhood—loving a father who'd barely known she'd existed, loving stepbrothers who'd laughed at her accent and resented her intrusion into their lives.

Then, of course, her relationship with James had confirmed it. One-sided love was not enough. Love had to flow both ways for it to work—or it did as far as she was concerned.

So here she was, like Cinderella heading for the ball, on the lookout for a prince.

Harry's a prince, her heart whispered, but she wasn't having any of that. Harry was gone, done and dusted, out of her life, and whatever other clichés might fit this new determination.

And if her chest hurt, well, that was to be expected. Limbs hurt after parts of them were amputated and getting Harry out of her heart was the same thing—an amputation.

But having confirmed this decision, shouldn't she take her own car to the wedding? She could use the excuse that she needed to be with Mrs P. Keeping Mrs P. calm and rational—or as calm and rational as an over-excitable Greek woman could manage on the day her only son was married—was Grace's job for the day.

A shiver of uncertainty worse, right now, than her worry over Harry feathered down Grace's spine. Mike's mother had planned this wedding with the precision of a military exercise—or perhaps a better comparison would be a full-scale, no-holds-barred, Technicolor, wide-screen movie production.

Thinking now of Mrs Poulos, Grace glanced towards the window. Was the wind getting up again? It sounded wild out there, although at the moment it wasn't raining. When the previous day had dawned bright and sunny, the hospital staff had let out their collective breaths. At least, it had seemed, Mrs P. would get her way with the weather.

But now?

The cyclone that had teased the citizens of North Queensland for days, travelling first towards the coast then veering away from it, had turned out to sea a few days earlier, there, everyone hoped, to spend its fury without any further damage. Here in Crocodile Creek, the river was rising, the bridge barely visible above the water, while the strong winds and rain earlier in the week had brought tree branches crashing down on houses, and Grace's SES workers had been kept busy, spreading tarpaulins over the damage.

Not that tarps would keep out the rain if the cyclone turned back their way—they'd be ripped off by the wind within minutes, along with the torn roofing they were trying to protect—

'Aren't you ready yet?'

Christina was calling from the living room, although Grace had given her and Joe the main bedroom—the bedroom they'd shared for a long time before moving to New Zealand to be closer to Joe's family. Now Grace rented the little cottage from Christina, and was hoping to discuss buying it while the couple was here for the birth of their first child as well as the hospital weddings.

'Just about,' she answered, taking a last look at herself and wondering again if she'd gone overboard with the new dress and the matching ribbon threaded through her short fair curls.

Wondering again about driving herself but thinking perhaps she'd left that decision too late. Harry would be here any minute. Besides, her friends might think she was snubbing them.

She'd just have to pretend—she was good at that—

only today, instead of pretending Harry was just a friend, she'd have to pretend that all was well between them. In a distant kind of way.

She certainly wasn't going to spoil Mike and Em's wedding by sulking over Harry all through it.

'Wow!'

Joe's slow smile told her he meant the word of praise, and Grace's doubts disappeared.

'Wow yourself,' she said, smiling at him. 'Christina's pregnant and you're the one that's glowing. You both look fantastic.'

She caught the private, joyous smile they shared and felt it pierce her heart like a shard of glass, but held her own smile firmly in place. She might know she'd lost her bounce—lost a little of her delight in life and all the wonders it had to offer—but she'd managed to keep it from being obvious to her friends. Still smiling, still laughing, still joking with her colleagues, hiding the pain of her pointless, unrequited love beneath her bubbly exterior.

Pretence!

'And you've lost weight,' Christina said, eyeing Grace more carefully now. 'Not that it doesn't suit you, you look beautiful, but don't go losing any more.'

'Beautiful? Grace O'Riordan beautiful? Pregnancy affecting your vision?' Grace said, laughing at her friends—mocking the warmth of pleasure she was feeling deep inside.

Harry heard the laugh as he took the two steps up to the cottage veranda in one stride. No one laughed like Grace, not as often or as—was 'musically' the right word? Grace's laugh sounded like the notes of a beautiful bird, cascading through the air, bringing pleasure to all who heard it.

Beautiful bird? Was all this wedding business turning him fanciful?

Surely not!

While as for Grace…

He caught the groan that threatened to escape his lips. He was in the right—he had no doubt about that. What he did and didn't do wasn't Grace's business. Yet he was uneasily aware that he'd upset her and wasn't quite sure how to fix things between them.

Wasn't, for reasons he couldn't fathom, entirely sure he wanted to…

At least it sounded as if they were ready. He'd offered to drive the three of them, thinking his big four-by-four would be more comfortable for the very pregnant Christina than Grace's little VW, but now he was regretting the impulse. With the possibility that the cyclone would turn back towards the coast, he had an excuse to avoid the wedding altogether, which would also mean not having to face Grace.

Although Mike had been a friend for a long time…

A sudden gust of wind brought down a frond from a palm tree and, super-sensitive right now to any change in the atmospheric conditions, Harry stopped, turned and looked around at the trees and shrubs in the cottage's garden. The wind had definitely picked up again, stripping leaves off the frangipani and bruising the delicate flowers. He shook his head, certain now the cyclone must have swung back towards them again, yet knowing there was nothing he, or anyone else, could do to stop it if it continued towards the coast this time.

They would just have to check all their preparations then wait and see. Preparations were easy—it was the waiting that was hard.

'You look as if you're off to a funeral, not a wedding,' Christina teased as she came out the door, and though he found a smile for her, it must have been too late, for she reached out and touched his arm, adding quietly, 'Weddings must be hard for you.'

He shook his head, rejecting her empathy—not deserving it, although she wasn't to know that. Then he looked beyond her and had to look again.

Was that really Grace?

And if it was, why was his body stirring?

Grace it was, smiling at him, a strained smile certainly, but recognisable as a smile, and saying something. Unfortunately, with his blood thundering in his ears, he couldn't hear the words, neither could he lip-read because his eyes kept shifting from her hair—a ribbon twined through golden curls—to her face—was it the colour of the dress that made her eyes seem bluer?—to her cleavage—more stirring—to a slim leg that was showing through a slit in the dark blue piece of fabric she seemed to have draped rather insecurely around her body.

His first instinct was to take off his jacket and cover her with it, his second was to hit Joe, who was hovering proprietorially behind her, probably looking down that cleavage.

He did neither, simply nodding to the pair before turning and leading the way out to the car, trying hard not to limp—he hated sympathy—opening the front door for Christina, explaining she'd be more comfortable there, letting Joe open the rear door for Grace, then regretting a move that put the pair of them together in the back seat.

Mental head slap! What was *wrong* with him? These three were his friends—good friends—Grace especially, even though, right now, he wasn't sure where he stood with Grace.

Very carefully, he tucked Christina's voluminous dress in around her, extended the seat belt so it would fit around her swollen belly, then shut the door, though not without a glance towards the back seat—towards Grace.

She was peering out the window, squinting upwards.

Avoiding looking at him?

He couldn't blame her.

But when she spoke he realised just how wrong he was. He was the last thing on Grace's mind.

'Look, there's a patch of blue sky. The sun *is* going to shine for Mike and Emily.'

Harry shook his head. That was a Grace he recognised, always thinking of others, willing the weather to be fine so her friends could be blessed with sunshine at their wedding.

Although that Grace usually wore big T-shirts and long shorts—that Grace, as far as he'd been aware, didn't have a cleavage…

Christina and Joe had both joined Grace in her study of the growing patch of blue sky, Christina sure having sunshine was a good omen for a happy marriage.

'Sunshine's good for the bride because her dress won't get all wet and her hair won't go floppy,' Joe declared, with all the authority of a man five months into marriage who now understood about women's hair and rain. 'But forget about omens—there's only one thing that will guarantee a happy marriage, and that's a willingness for both partners to work at it.'

He slid a hand onto Christina's shoulder then added, 'Harry here knows that.'

Grace saw the movement of Harry's shoulders as he winced, and another shard of glass pierced her vulnerable heart. She hadn't been working at the hospital when Harry's wife, Nikki, had died, but she'd heard enough to know of his devotion to her—of the endless hours he'd spent by her side—and of his heartbreak at her death.

You're not my wife!

The words intruded on her sympathy but she ignored them, determined to pretend that all was well between them—at least in front of other people.

'What's the latest from the weather bureau, Harry?' she asked, hoping to divert his mind from memories she was sure would be bad enough on someone else's wedding day. 'Does this wind mean Willie's turned again and is heading back our way, or is it the early warning of another storm?'

He glanced towards her in the rear-view vision mirror and nodded as if to say, I know what you're doing. But his spoken reply was crisply matter-of-fact. 'Willie's turned—he's running parallel to the coast again but at this stage the bureau has no indication of whether he'll turn west towards us or continue south. The winds are stronger because he's picked up strength—upgraded from a category three to a category four in the last hour.'

'I wouldn't like to think he'll swing around to the west,' Joe said anxiously, obviously worried about being caught in a cyclone with a very pregnant wife.

'He's been so unpredictable he could do anything,' Harry told him. 'And even if he doesn't head our way, we're in for floods as the run-off further upstream comes down the creek.'

'Well, at least we're in the right place—at a hospital,' Christina said. 'And look, isn't that sunshine peeking through the clouds?'

Harry had pulled up in the parking lot of the church, set in a curve of the bay in the main part of town. Christina was right. One ray of sunshine had found its way through a weakness in the massed, roiling clouds, reflecting its golden light off the angry grey-brown ocean that heaved and roared and crashed into the cove beneath the headland where Mike's parents' restaurant, the Athina, stood.

He watched the ray of light play on the thunderous waves and knew Joe was right—omens like that meant nothing as far as happiness was concerned. The sun had shone on his and Nikki's wedding day—for all the good it had done.

Grace felt her spirits lift with that single ray of light. Her friends were getting married, she was looking good, and so what if Harry Blake didn't want her worrying about him? This was her chance to look at other men and maybe find one who might, eventually, share her dreams of a family.

Unfortunately, just as she was reminding herself of her intention to look around at the single wedding guests, Harry opened the car door for her, and as she slid out a sudden wind gust ripped the door from his hands and only his good reflexes in grabbing her out of the way saved her from being hit by it.

It was hard to think about other men with Harry's strong arm wrapped around her, holding her close to his chest. Hard to think about anything when she was dealing with her own private storm—the emotional one—raging within *her* chest.

You're not my wife.

He's done and dusted.

She pulled away, annoyed with herself for reacting as she had, but determined to hide how she felt. He'd taken her elbow to guide her across the windswept parking lot outside the church and was acting as if nothing untoward had occurred between them. He was even pretending not to limp, which was just as well because she had no intention of asking him how his leg was. Because, Mr Policeman, two could play the pretend game.

She smiled up at him.

'Isn't this fun?'

Harry stared at her in disbelief.

Fun?

For a start, he was riven with guilt over his behaviour the previous night, and on top of that, the person he considered—or had considered up until last night—his best friend had turned into a sexpot.

That was fun?

Sexpot? Where on earth had he got that word?

He cast another glance towards his companion—golden hair gleaming in the sunlight, the freckles on her nose sparkling like gold dust, cleavage…

Yep. Sexpot.

'You OK?'

Even anxious, she looked good enough to eat.

Slowly…

Mouthful by sexy mouthful…

'Fine,' he managed to croak, denying the way his body was behaving, wondering if rain had the same effect cold showers were purported to have.

Although the rain appeared to have gone…

Bloody cyclones—never around when you needed them.

'Oh, dear, there's Mrs P. and she looks distraught.' Grace's voice broke into this peculiar reverie.

'Did you expect her to be anything but?' he asked, as Grace left his side and hurried towards the woman who was wringing her hands and staring up towards the sky.

'I'm on mother-in-law watch,' Grace explained, smiling back over her shoulder at him. Maybe they *were* still friends. 'I promised Em I'd try to keep Mrs P. calm.'

Harry returned her smile just in case the damage done was not irreparable.

'About as easy as telling the cyclone not to change course,' he said, before hurrying after Christina and Joe.

Grace carried his smile with her as she walked towards Mrs Poulos, although she knew Harry's smiles, like the polite way Harry would take someone's elbow to cross a road, were part of the armour behind which he hid all his emotions.

And she was through with loving Harry anyway.

Mrs P. was standing beside the restaurant's big catering van, though what it was doing there when the reception was at the restaurant, Grace couldn't fathom.

'What's the problem, Mrs P.?' Grace asked as she approached, her sympathy for the woman whose plans had been thrown into chaos by the weather clear in her voice.

'Oh, Grace, it's the doves. I don't know what to do about the doves.'

'Doves?' Grace repeated helplessly, clasping the hyperventilating woman around the shoulders and patting her arm, telling her to breathe deeply.

'The doves—how can I let them fly?' Mrs P. wailed, lifting her arms to the heavens, as if doves might suddenly descend.

Grace looked around, seeking someone who might explain this apparent disaster. But although a figure in white was hunched behind the wheel of the delivery van, whoever it was had no intention of helping.

'The dove man phoned,' Mrs P. continued. 'He says they will blow away in all this wind. They will never get home. They will die.'

'Never get home' provided a slight clue. Grace had heard of homing pigeons—weren't doves just small pigeons?

Did they home?

'Just calm down and we'll think about it,' she told Mrs P. 'Breathe deeply, then tell me about the doves.'

But the mention of the birds sent Mrs Poulos back into paroxysms of despair, which stopped only when Grace reminded her they had a bare ten minutes until the ceremony began—ten minutes before she had to be ready in her special place as mother of the groom.

'But the doves?'

Mrs P. pushed past Grace, and opened the rear doors of the van. And there, in a large crate with a wire netting front, were, indeed, doves.

Snowy white, they strutted around behind the wire, heads tipping to one side as their bright, inquisitive eyes peered out at the daylight.

'They were to be my special surprise,' Mrs P. explained, poking a finger through the wire to stroke the feathers of the closest bird. 'I had it all arranged. Albert, who is our new trainee chef, he was going to release them just as Mike and Emily came out of the church. They are trained, you know, the doves. They know to circle the happy couple three times before they take off.'

And heaven only knows what they'll do as they circle three times, Grace thought, imagining the worst. But saving Em from bird droppings wasn't her job— keeping Mrs Poulos on an even keel was.

'It was a wonderful idea,' Grace told the older woman. 'And it would have looked magical, but you're right about the poor things not being able to fly home in this wind. We'll just have to tell Mike and Emily about it later.'

'But their happiness,' Mrs P. protested. 'We need to do the doves to bring them happiness.'

She was calmer now but so determined Grace understood why Emily had agreed to the plethora of attendants Mrs P. had arranged, and the fluffy tulle creations all the female members of the wedding party had been pressed into wearing. Mrs P. had simply worn Em down—ignoring any suggestions and refusing to countenance any ideas not her own.

'We could do it later,' Mrs P. suggested. 'Maybe when Mike and Emily cut the cake and kiss. Do you think we can catch the doves afterwards if we let them out inside the restaurant? All the doors and windows are shut because of the wind so they wouldn't get out. Then we could put them back in their box and everything will be all right.'

Grace flicked her attention back to the cage, and counted.

Ten!

Ten birds flying around inside a restaurant packed with more than one hundred guests? A dozen dinner-jacketed waiters chasing fluttering doves?

And Em was worried the sea of tulle might make a farce of things!

'No!' Grace said firmly. 'We can't have doves flying around inside the restaurant.'

She scrambled around in her head for a reason, knowing she'd need something forceful.

More than forceful…

'CJ, Cal and Gina's little boy—he's one of the pages, isn't he?' She crossed her fingers behind her back before she told her lie. 'Well, he's very allergic to bird feathers. Think how terrible it would be if we had to clear a table and use a steak knife to do an emergency tracheotomy on him—you know, one of those opera-tions where you have to cut a hole in the throat so the person can breathe. Think how terrible that would be in the middle of the reception.'

Mrs Poulos paled, and though she opened her mouth to argue, she closed it again, finally nodding agreement.

'And we'd get feathers on the cake,' she added, and

Grace smiled. Now it was Mrs P.'s idea not to have the doves cavorting inside the restaurant, one disaster had been averted.

Gently but firmly Grace guided her charge towards the church, finally settling her beside her husband in the front pew.

'Doves?' Mr Poulos whispered to Grace above his wife's head, and Grace nodded.

'No doves,' she whispered back, winning a warm smile of appreciation.

She backed out of the pew, her job done for now, and was making her way towards the back of the church, where she could see friends sitting, when Joe caught her arm.

'We've kept a seat for you,' he said, ushering her in front of him towards a spare place between Christina and Harry.

Sitting through a wedding ceremony beside Harry was hardly conducive to amputating him out of her heart.

Although the way things were between them, he might shift to another pew. Or, manlike, had he moved on from the little scene last night—the entire episode forgotten?

Grace slid into the seat, apprehension tightening ever sinew in her body, so when Harry shifted and his sleeve brushed her arm, she jerked away.

'Problems?' Harry whispered, misreading her reaction.

'All sorted,' she whispered back, but a flock of doves circling around inside the restaurant paled into insignificance beside the turmoil within her body.

Remembering her own advice to Mrs P., Grace closed her eyes and breathed deeply.

Harry watched her breasts rise and fall, and wondered just how badly he'd hurt her with his angry words. Or was something else going on that he didn't know about? He glanced around, but apart from flowers and bows and a lot of pink and white frothy drapery everything appeared normal. Mike was ready by the altar, and a change in the background music suggested Emily was about to make an appearance.

So why was Grace as tense as fencing wire?

She'd seemed OK earlier, as if determined to pretend everything was all right between them—at least for the duration of the wedding.

So it had to be something else.

Did she not like weddings?

Had something terrible happened in her past, something connected with a wedding?

The thought of something terrible happening in Grace's past made him reach out and take her hand, thinking, at the same time, how little he knew of her.

Her fingers were cold and they trembled slightly, making him want to hug her reassuringly, but things were starting, people standing up, kids in shiny dresses and suits were scattering rose petals, and a confusion of young women in the same pink frothy stuff that adorned the church were parading down the aisle. Emily, he assumed, was somewhere behind them, because Mike's face had lit up with a smile so soppy Harry felt a momentary pang of compassion for him.

Poor guy had it bad!

Beside him Grace sighed—or maybe sniffed—and

he turned away from the wedding party, sorting itself with some difficulty into the confined space in front of the altar, and looked at the woman by his side.

'Are you crying?' he demanded, his voice harsher than he'd intended because anxiety had joined the stirring thing that was happening again in his body.

Grace smiled up at him, easing the anxiety but exacerbating the stirring.

'No way,' she said. 'I was thinking of the last wedding I was at.'

'Bad?'

She glanced his way and gave a nod.

'My father's fourth. He introduced me to the latest Mrs O'Riordan as Maree's daughter. My mother's name was Kirstie.'

No wonder Grace looked grim.

And how it must have hurt.

But her father's fourth marriage?

Did that explain why Grace had never married?

'His fourth? Has his example put you off marriage for life?'

No smile, but she did turn towards him, studying him for a moment before replying, this time with a very definite shake of her head.

'No way, but I do feel a trifle cynical about the celebratory part. If ever I get married, I'll elope.'

'No pink and white frothy dresses?' he teased, hoping, in spite of the stirring, she'd smile again.

Hoping smiles might signal all was well between them once again.

'Not a froth in sight! And I think it's peach, not pink,' she said, and did smile.

But the smile was sad somehow, and a little part of him wondered just how badly having a marriage-addicted father might have hurt her.

He didn't like the idea of Grace hurting…

Handling this well, Grace congratulated herself. Strangely enough, the impersonal way Harry had taken her hand had helped her settle down. But just in case this settling effect turned to something else, she gently detached her hand from his as they stood up. And although he'd put his arm around her shoulders and given her a hug, it was definitely a friend kind of a hug and had reminded her that's what she was to him.

Now all she had to do was close her mind to the words being spoken at the front, pretend that Harry was nothing more to her than the friend she was to him, and keep an eye on Mrs P. in case she thought of some new reason for panic.

Fun!

It *was* fun, Grace decided, some hours later.

True, Harry had excused himself and left the church not long after the ceremony began, but whether because he couldn't bear to sit through it or to check on the latest weather report and weather-related incidents, she didn't know. Something had certainly happened—tiles or something coming off the roof—because there'd been loud crashing noises then the minister had insisted everyone leave through the vestry, disrupting the wedding party to the extent Grace had to calm Mrs P. down once again, persuading her the wedding was still legal even if the happy couple hadn't left as man and wife through the front door of the church.

Grace had driven to the restaurant with Mr and Mrs Poulos so hadn't caught up with Christina and Joe until the reception.

People milled around, sipping champagne, talking and even dancing. Luke Bresciano came up to her, took the champagne glass out of her hand, set it down on a handy table, and swept her onto the dance floor.

'I was looking for you,' he said, guiding her carefully around the floor. 'Have you heard the ink-blot joke? I remembered it after we looked at the stain last night.'

Grace shook her head, and Luke launched into the story of the psychologist showing ink-blot pictures to a patient.

'So the fellow looks at the first one, and says that's two rabbits having sex. The psychologist turns the page and the fellow says, that's an elephant and a rhino having sex. The psychologist is a bit shocked but he offers a third. That's three people and a dog having sex. Floored by this reaction, the psychologist loses his cool. "You've got a dirty mind," he tells his patient. "Me?" the patient says. "You're the one showing filthy pictures."'

Grace laughed, looking more closely at this man she barely knew. The lines around his eyes suggested he was older than she knew he was. Signs of the unhappiness she'd heard was in his background?

She asked about his early life but somehow the questions ended up coming from him, so by the end of the dance she knew no more than she had at the beginning.

Except that he had a sense of humour, which was a big point in his favour.

But when she glimpsed Harry across the room,

bending down to speak to Charles, the excited beating of her heart told her she had a long way to go in the getting over him stakes. Fortunately the best man— some friend of Mike's who'd come across from New Zealand—appeared and asked her to dance, so Harry was not forgotten but tucked away behind her determination to move on.

The dance ended, and she noticed Harry heading in her direction. Dancing with Harry was *not* part of the plan, so she picked up her glass of now flat champagne and pressed into an alcove of pot plants, hoping to hide in this corner of the greenery festooning the restaurant.

Could one hide from a policeman?

'You know I can't dance with my leg!'

It wasn't exactly the greeting she'd expected. In fact, the slightly petulant statement made no sense whatsoever.

'What are you talking about? What do you mean?' she demanded, looking up into Harry's face, which seemed to be flushed with the same anger she'd heard in his voice.

'That I can't dance with you,' he said, his words as cross as his first statement had been.

'Then it's just as well I'm not your mother or your wife,' Grace retorted, unable to keep up the 'friends' pretence another second. 'Because if I was, you'd be expected to dance with me.'

She tried to turn away but the greenery defeated her—the greenery and Harry's hand on her shoulder.

'I shouldn't have said that to you,' he said, tightening his grip when she tried to shrug it off. 'I'm sorry.'

Grace looked at him for a long moment. The flush

had faded, leaving his face pale and so tired-looking she had to sternly stem the flash of sympathy she felt towards him.

'No,' she told him, knowing this was the perfect time to begin to distance herself from Harry. 'I think it needed to be said. You were right, it's not my place to tell you what to do or what not to do. I overstepped the boundaries of friendship but it won't happen again, I promise you.'

Harry stared at her, totally befuddled by what had just occurred. Hadn't he apologised? Said what had to be said to make things right again between himself and Grace? So why was she rejecting his apology? Or, if not rejecting it, turning things so it had been her fault, not his?

He opened him mouth but what could he say? *Please, keep telling me stuff like that? Please, stay concerned for me?*

Ridiculous!

He should let it go—walk away—and hope everything would come right between them in time.

Hope they could go back to being friends.

But if he walked away she'd dance with someone else, and seeing Grace in that Italian doctor's arms, laughing up at some funny thing he'd said, had made Harry's gut churn.

'I can shuffle if you don't mind a shuffling kind of dance,' he heard himself say, and saw astonishment similar to what he was feeling reflected on Grace's face.

Her 'OK' wasn't overwhelmingly enthusiastic, but he was happy to settle for even grudging acceptance.

He put his arms around her, tucked her body close to his, and felt her curls tickle the skin beneath his chin.

Grace knew this wouldn't do much for her distancing-Harry plans, but surely a woman was allowed a little bit of bliss. She slid into his arms and put her arms around his back—allowable, she was sure, because it was going to be a shuffling kind of dance.

You are stupid, the sensible voice in her head muttered at her.

It's just pretence, she told her head. Everything else seemed to be about pretence these days so why not pretend, just for a short while, that they were a couple? After all, she could go back to distancing tomorrow.

It was heaven.

The band was playing a slow waltz, or maybe a slow two-step. Dancing was something she did naturally but had little knowledge about, and she and Harry were at the edge of the dance floor, barely moving to the music, content, as far as Grace was concerned, just to be in each other's arms.

What Harry was thinking was a mystery but, then, Harry in a social setting—apart from coffee at the pub—was something of a mystery as well.

No matter—he had his arms around her and that was enough.

Well, nearly enough. Outside the wind had gathered strength again and rain lashed the garden beyond the restaurant and flung itself against the windows. It was definitely 'snuggling closer' weather. If she moved just slightly she could rest her head against his chest, and for a little while she could dream.

Later, she couldn't remember whether she'd actually

made this daring move or not, but what she did remember was that the lights went out, then Harry spun her around, into even denser blackness in a corner of the restaurant.

And bent his head.

And kissed her.

Harry kissed her…

Folded in his arms, her curls tickling at his chin, Harry had ignored the cleavage as much as possible as he'd shuffled back and forth with this different Grace on the corner of the dance floor. But when the lights went out, he lost the slim reins of control he'd been clinging to and whisked her into the shadows of one of the palms that dotted the restaurant.

He bent his head, and kissed her, curls first, then her forehead, finding the salt of perspiration on her skin and a sweetness he knew by instinct was pure Grace.

His lips moved to her temples, felt the throb of a vein, then claimed her mouth, more sweetness, but this time mingled with heat as Grace responded with a fire that lit his own smouldering desire, so need and hunger fought common sense and a determination to not get involved.

A losing battle—as useless as trying to stop the wind that now raged again outside—as useless as trying to stop a cyclone…

He clamped Grace's curvy body hard against his leanness, and drank in the taste of her as his mouth explored and challenged hers. She met his challenge and responded with her own, so he was lost in the wonder and sweetness and fire that was this new Grace.

Gripped in the toils of physical attraction, a voice whispered in his head, but he ignored it and kept kissing the woman in his arms.

Lamplight. Flickering candles. Maybe the voice wasn't in his head. Someone was calling his name.

Urgently.

'Harry Blake.'

CHAPTER THREE

CHARLES WETHERBY, the wheelchair-bound head of the hospital, was illuminated by candelabrum, held aloft by a young policeman, Troy Newton, the newest member of Harry's staff.

'Charles?'

Harry eased Grace gently away, tucking her, he hoped, into deeper shadows, and took the two long strides needed to bring him close to Charles.

'Bus accident up on the mountain road—road's subsided and the bus has slid down the mountain. Dan Macker called it in.'

'Do we know exactly where, and who's on the way?' Harry asked, looking towards the windows and knowing there was no way the rescue helicopter, based at the hospital, could fly in this wind.

'Where? This side of Dan's place. He saw the bus go past, then later heard a noise, and when he investigated he saw the landslide. Who's on the way? The fire truck, two ambulances each with two crew and the hospital's four-wheel-drive is on its way here to pick up whatever hospital staff you think you might need on site. Have you seen Grace? If we've got to set up a triage post and then get people off the side of the mountain, we'll probably need an SES crew up there as well—she can organise that.'

'I'll tell her,' Harry said, 'and head out there myself.'

Charles made an announcement aimed mainly at the hospital staff, telling them the hospital would go to the code black disaster plan, then Harry spoke, reminding people who would be taking part in the rescue on the mountain that there were open diggings and mine shafts on the slopes, legacy of the gold rush that had led to the birth of the township that had become Crocodile Creek.

He looked around the room, wondering who he'd take, picking out hospital staff he knew were fit and active, telling them to take the hospital vehicle while he'd check on his other staff and be right behind them.

He turned back towards the shadows but Grace had gone, no doubt because she'd heard the news. More candles had been lit, but it was impossible to pick her out in the milling crowd. Joe touched his arm.

'You go, I'll organise a lift back to the cottage for Grace and Christina then go up to the hospital to see if I can help.'

Harry nodded to Joe but his eyes still searched for Grace, although common sense told him she'd be in a corner somewhere, on her mobile, starting a phone relay to gather a crew at SES headquarters in the shortest possible time. Then she'd head to the headquarters herself to organise the equipment they'd need.

As he left the restaurant, striding towards his vehicle, that thought brought with it a sense of relief he didn't quite understand. Was it tied up with the fact that Grace was safer at headquarters, organising things, than on the side of a slippery mountain riddled with old mineshafts, fighting cyclonic winds in pitch darkness?

Surely not!

Although, as a friend, he was entitled to feel some concern for her safety, so it had nothing to do with the aberration in his feelings towards her—which was purely physical.

The wind was now so strong he had to struggle to open the car door—memories of a soft body held against his chest...

Get your mind focussed on the job!

He started the car and turned out of the car park, concentrating on driving through the lashing wind and rain.

Ignoring the physical aberration? That was the voice in his head again.

Of course he was ignoring it. What else could he do? Physical attraction had led him into a terrible mistake once before and had caused pain and unhappiness, not only to himself but to Nikki as well. It had flung him into an emotional swamp so deep and damaging he'd blocked emotion out of his life ever since.

So there was no way he could allow whatever physical attraction he might be feeling towards her to touch his friendship with Grace.

If he still had a friendship with Grace. Her words before the dance had indicated she was backing away from whatever it was they'd had.

Yet she'd kissed him back—he was sure of that.

He'd have to put it aside—forget about the kiss and definitely forget about the lust he'd felt towards his friend.

Determinedly setting these thoughts aside, Harry

drove cautiously down towards the town, automatically noting the level of the water beneath the bridge, forcing himself to think rescue not Grace.

He had to go, of course he did, Grace told herself as she watched Harry leave. She was on the phone to Paul Gibson, still the nominal head of the local SES, although since he'd been undergoing treatment for prostate cancer, Grace, as senior team leader, had taken over a lot of his responsibilities. But Paul's knowledge and experience were still invaluable, so Grace forgot about Harry and listened, mentally repeating all Paul had said so she'd remember.

Rolls of netting—she'd seen them in the big shed and often wondered about them—were useful in land-slides. You could anchor them on the level ground and unroll them down the slope to make it easier for rescuers to clamber up and down.

'Belongings,' Paul continued. 'Gather up what you can of people's belongings. They're going to be disoriented enough, ending up in a strange hospital—if we can return things to them, it helps. And remember to search for a hundred yards all around the bus—people can wander off. As soon as my wife gets back from checking on the family, I'll get her to drive me up to Headquarters. I mightn't be much use out in the field, but I'll handle the radio calls and relays up there, which will leave you free to be out in the field.'

Through the window Grace saw Harry's big vehicle leave the car park.

'Thanks, Paul,' she said, staring out the window at the vehicle, hope sneaking in where wonder and amazement had been.

Harry had kissed her.

Surely he wouldn't have done that if he wasn't interested in her?

The sneaky scrap of hope swelled like a balloon to fill her chest.

Maybe, just maybe, she wouldn't have to get over Harry after all.

Or was she being stupid? The way she'd been with James? Thinking flowers and dinners out and a physical relationship meant love?

Not that she'd had any of that with Harry. Only one interrupted kiss.

The balloon deflated as fast as it had filled, leaving her feeling empty and flat.

One thing she knew for sure—she'd been stupid for kissing him back, for letting her lips tell him things her head knew she couldn't tell him.

She tucked her phone back into her beaded handbag and looked around the room, checking who was leaving, who might give her a lift home so she could change before going to Headquarters. Charles was leading the way out the door, Jill Shaw, director of nursing, moving more slowly to guide Susie, who was swinging along on crutches, thanks to her accident the previous day.

'Would you lot drop me home?' Grace asked, coming up to them. 'I can hardly organise my crew dressed like this.'

'No problem,' Charles told her, while Jill, who must have been running through the nursing roster in her head, added, 'You're off duty until Tuesday, aren't you, Grace?'

Grace nodded. Her month on night duty had finished at seven that morning and the change in shift meant she had three days off.

'But I grabbed a few hours' sleep this morning so I'm happy to be called in. If Willie's really heading back towards us, we'll need all available staff standing by.'

'We might need all staff back on duty, not standing by, if the bus that's come off the mountain had a full load of passengers,' Charles said, as the women ducked behind his wheelchair to escape some of the wind that was ripping across the car park, grabbing at Charles's words and flinging them into the air. 'With this weather, we can't fly people out, and at last report the coast road was flooding. We could have a very full hospital.'

Jill confirmed this with a quiet 'I'll be in touch' as she dropped Grace at the cottage, but nursing was forgotten as Grace stripped off her dress and clambered into her bright orange SES overalls, fitted on the belt that held her torch, pocket knife and radio then grabbed her keys and headed for Headquarters. The crews would be gathering. She'd send one support vehicle straight up the mountain, and hold the second one back until she heard from Harry in case some special equipment not on the main rescue vehicle was needed.

Or…

She went herself, with the first crew, partly because Paul had arrived to handle the office but also because she knew an extra person with nursing skills would be useful in the rescue mission. This truck held the inflatable tent they'd use for triage and the generator that kept it inflated. They'd have to make sure the tent was anchored securely in this wind.

The men and women chatted casually, but Grace, huddled in a corner, mentally rehearsed the jobs that lay ahead as she watched the wind slice rain across the windscreen and cause the vehicle to sway from side to side. Willie had turned and was heading their way—the cyclone warnings on the radio had confirmed what increased velocity in the wind had already told most locals.

How much time did they have to get ready?

Who would need to be moved from their homes? An evacuation list would have been drawn up but before she, or anyone else, could start moving people to safety, they had to get the accident victims off the mountain...

'Your crews finished?'

Grace was kneeling by a young woman, the last person to be pulled from the bus after the jaws of life had been used to free her. Unconscious and with probable head injuries, she lay on an undamaged part of the road, her neck in a collar, her body strapped to the cradle stretcher on which she'd been pulled up the muddy slope. Now, as the wind howled around them, they awaited the return of one of the ambulances that had been shuttling back and forth to the hospital for hours.

About half an hour earlier, once most of the accident victims had been moved out of it and ferried down the mountain, Harry had deemed the inflatable tent too dangerous. So Grace's crew had packed it and the generator back into the SES truck prior to departure.

A makeshift shelter remained to protect this final patient, but the wind was getting stronger every minute and now blew rain and forest debris beneath the sodden tarpaulin. Grace had angled her body so it shielded the young woman's face. She smoothed the woman's hair and removed leaves that blew onto her skin, but there was little else she could do for her—just watch and wait, holding her hand and talking quietly to her, because Grace was certain even unconscious people had some awareness.

'Are your crews finished?'

As Harry repeated his question, Grace turned to look at him. She'd heard him the first time but her mind had been too busy adjusting to his abrupt tone—and trying to work out what it meant—for her to answer.

'Just about,' she said, searching his face, lit by the last emergency light, for some hint of his mood. Disappointment because they'd failed to save the bus driver? No, deep down Harry might be gutted, but he would set it aside until the job was done.

Was his leg hurting?

It had to be, though if she offered sympathy it was sure to be rejected.

She stopped guessing about his mood, and explained, 'One of the team is already on its way back to base and the other is packing up the gear and should be leaving shortly. Why?'

'Because I want everyone off the mountain, that's why,' Harry said, his voice straining against the wind, but Grace's attention was back on her patient.

'She's stopped breathing.'

Grace leant forward over the young woman, tilted her head backwards then lifted her chin upward with one hand to make sure her airway was clear, and felt for a pulse with the other. Her fingers pushed beneath the woman's chin, and found a flutter of movement in the carotid artery.

She stripped off the oxygen mask and gave the woman two breaths, then checked the pulse again. Looked at Harry, who was now squatting by her side.

'You monitor her pulse—I'll breathe.'

They'd practised so often as a team, it seemed effortless now, Grace breathing, Harry monitoring the young woman's vital signs. Yet it was taking too long—were their efforts in vain?

'We'll get her,' Harry said, and the conviction in his voice comforted Grace, although she knew he couldn't be as certain as he sounded.

Or could he?

Grace stopped, and held her breath. The rise and fall of the young woman's chest told them she'd resumed breathing on her own.

'Yes!' Grace said, lifting her hand for a high-five of triumph, but Harry's hands were by his side, and the bleak unhappiness on his face was far from triumph.

Whatever pretence at friendship they'd managed during the wedding was gone.

Burnt away by the heat of that kiss?

Though why would *he* be upset over the kiss? Because it had broken some rule he'd set himself when his wife died?

Thou shalt kiss no other after her?

That was weird because Harry wasn't stupid and he must know that eventually nature would reassert itself and he'd want a sexual relationship with some woman—sometime.

Although as far as she knew, monks didn't…

'I want you off the mountain,' he said.

'I want us all off the mountain,' Grace retorted, battling to understand his mood. OK, he was worried about the cyclone, but they all were, and it certainly hadn't made the other rescuers go all brisk and formal. In fact, the others had made an effort to smile even as they'd struggled up the steepest parts of the slope— everyone encouraging each other.

All but Harry, who'd frowned at Grace whenever they'd passed, as if he couldn't understand who she was or perhaps what she was doing there.

'But that's hardly possible,' she continued crisply, 'without magic carpets to whisk us all away. The second SES crew will be leaving soon. The rest of the hospital personnel have gone back to deal with the patients as they arrive. I'm staying with this patient and I'll go back in the ambulance when it gets here.'

'This place is dangerous. The wind's increasing all the time. More of the road could slip, trees could come down.'

He was worrying about her safety. That was the only explanation for Harry's strange behaviour. The thought brought such warmth to Grace's body she forgot about distancing herself. She forgot about the cruel words he'd flung at her, and reached out to touch his arm.

'This is my job,' she said softly. 'We've had the risk-taking conversation, Harry, and while you mightn't like me talking about it you have to admit, as part of your job, you do it all the time. So you should understand I can't just get in the truck and go back to town, leaving this young woman with no one.'

'*I'm* here!' Harry said, moving his arm so her hand slid off—squelching the warmth.

It had been such a stupid thing to say Grace didn't bother with a reply. She checked the oxygen flowing into the mask that was once again covering the young woman's mouth and nose, and kept a hand on the pulse at her wrist.

Harry stood up and walked away, no doubt to grump at someone else. But who else was still here? Grace had no idea, having seen the last of the SES crew heading down the road towards their truck. The first truck had taken a lot of the less badly injured passengers back to the hospital to be checked under more ideal conditions than an inflatable tent and arclamps in lashing wind and rain. The team leader of that truck would then assist in finding accommodation for those not admitted to hospital, while the other members would begin preparations for the arrival of Willie, now on course to cross the coast at Crocodile Creek.

'That you, Grace?'

She turned at the shout and saw two overalled figures jogging towards her.

'Mike! Not on your honeymoon, then?'

Mike Poulos, newly married helicopter pilot and paramedic, reached her first and knelt beside her patient.

'Could hardly leave without Em, who's in Theatre as we speak, so I decided I might as well make myself useful. I can't fly in this weather but I still remember how to drive an ambulance. Who's this?'

'We don't know,' Grace told him, watching the gentle

way he touched the young woman's cheek. 'Maybe a young backpacker—there were quite a few young people among the passengers. No one seems to know for certain who was on the bus.'

'Mainly because the driver was killed and we can't find a manifest in the wreckage.' Harry was back, nodding to the two paramedics as he explained. 'This patient's the last, but we need to take the driver's body back to the hospital.'

'She's unconscious?' Mike asked Grace, who nodded.

'And though there are no obvious injuries, she's very unstable. She stopped breathing after she was brought up from the bus,' Grace told him.

'I hate transporting a dead person with a live one, but the bus driver deserves the dignity of an ambulance,' Mike said. He looked towards Harry.

'If we take the bus driver, can you take Grace?'

Harry looked doubtful.

'As against leaving me up here all night? Taking two patients means I won't fit in the ambulance,' Grace snapped at him, aggravated beyond reason by this stranger in Harry's body.

'I'll take Grace,' he conceded, then he led the two men away to collect the driver's body, before returning for Grace's patient.

Grace walked beside the young woman as the men carried her to the ambulance, then watched as she was loaded, the doors shut, and the big four-by-four vehicle took off down the road.

'My car's this way,' Harry said, and strode off into the darkness. He was carrying the last of the lights and the tarpaulin they'd used as a shelter, and though he looked overladen he'd shaken his head when had Grace asked if she could carry something.

Still puzzling over his strange behaviour, she followed him down the road to where it widened enough for a helicopter to land—*when* weather permitted. His was the only vehicle still there.

She waited while he stacked the gear he'd carried into the back, then she made her way to the passenger side, opened the door—no chivalry now—and climbed in.

'What is with you?' she demanded, as soon as he was settled into the driver's seat. 'Is your leg hurting? Should I have a look at it?'

He glanced towards her, his face carefully blank, then looked away to turn the key in the ignition, release the brake and start driving cautiously down the wind- and rain-lashed road.

'My leg's fine.'

Grace knew that was a lie—it couldn't possibly be fine—but she wasn't his mother or his wife so she kept her mouth shut.

Between them the radio chattered—the ambulance giving the hospital an ETA, a squad car reporting on more power lines down. Yet the noise barely intruded into the taut, chilly atmosphere that lay between the two of them as they crawled at a snail's pace down the mountain road.

'Is it the bus driver? I know there's nothing worse than losing a life at an accident, but he'd have been dead the moment the bus rolled on him, poor guy. There was nothing anyone could have done, and from what the rescuers were saying, he did all he could to save the bus from being more badly damaged—all he could to save more lives.'

'So he dies a hero. Do you think that makes it better for his kids? His name was Peter. He had two kids. Photo in his wallet.'

Making him a person in Harry's eyes. No wonder he was upset.

'Someone's father,' Grace whispered, feeling the rush of pity such information always brought, but at the same time she wondered about Harry's reaction. She'd seen him bring in dead kids from car accidents without this much emotional involvement. 'No, I'm sure, at the beginning at least, the hero stuff won't make a scrap of difference to two kids growing up without a father. But all we can do is help the living, Harry. We can't change what's past.'

Harry sighed.

'You're right, and if I think rationally about it, the simple fact of having a father is no guarantee of happiness,' he said glumly. 'Georgie's Max—his father's just a nasty waste of space—and yours doesn't sound as if he brought you much joy.'

'It might not have been all his fault. I kind of got dumped on him,' Grace told him, defending blood ties automatically. 'I didn't ever know him as a small child, then, when I was seven, my mother died and my aunt got in touch with my father, who'd emigrated from Ireland to Australia, and I was sent out here.'

She paused, remembering the small sad child who'd set off on that long journey, scared but somehow, beyond the fear, full of hope. She'd lost her mother, but ahead had lain a father and a new family, a father who'd surely love her or why else had he sent the money for her ticket?

'What number wife was he on at that stage?' Harry asked, and Grace smiled.

'Only number two, but, looking back, I think the marriage was probably teetering at the time and my stepmother had only agreed to take me because she thought it might keep my father with her. Poor woman, she was kind, but she was stuck with me when he took off again, so to her I always represented a terrible time of her life. And the little boys, my stepbrothers, well, I can't blame them for hating me—I arrive and their father leaves. In their young minds there had to be a connection.'

'No one could have hated you, Grace,' Harry said, but although the words were kind his harsh voice suggested that there was more than the dead bus driver bothering him.

She listened to the radio calls, not knowing what to guess at next, but certain she needed things sorted out between them because the success of both the preparations for, and the work after, Willie's arrival depended on them working harmoniously together.

With a sigh nearly as strong as one of the wind gusts outside, she tried again.

'Is that all that's bothering you? The bus driver? His kids?'

He turned to look at her and even in the dimly lit cabin she could read incredulity.

'We're in a serious situation here,' Harry said, spacing the words as if he'd had to test each one in his head before letting it out.

'We've been in serious situations before, Harry,' Grace reminded him, ducking instinctively as a tree-fern frond careened towards her side of the car. 'Remember the time we went out to the reef in a thunderstorm to rescue the diver with the bends? That wasn't serious?'

No comment.

Grace sighed again.

Was she becoming a sigher?

Surely not. And if she considered it, being at odds with Harry could only help her getting-over-him decision. A sensible woman would welcome this new attitude of his and get on with her life. But this was, as Harry had just pointed out, a serious situation and Grace knew she wouldn't give of her best if there was added tension between the two of them.

She knew too that they'd be in some dangerous situations in the future, and if they didn't have one hundred per cent attention on the job, a dangerous situation could become a disaster.

She had to sort it out.

But how?

Bluntly!

There was only one other thing that had happened this evening that could explain his attitude.

Or maybe two things.

'Are you still annoyed about me nagging you to be careful?' she asked, thinking it was easier to bring this up than to mention the kiss.

'I apologised for that.'

More silence.

That left the kiss.

Grace's last remnant of hope that the kiss might have meant something to Harry died.

For sure, he'd started it, but the worst of it was, she'd kissed him back.

She knew it had been a mistake from her side of things, but had it also worried Harry? Had she revealed too much of how she felt?

Was that what was bothering him?

If so, she had to get around it somehow. Act as if it had meant nothing to her—pretend it had been nothing more than a casual smooch in the darkness.

More pretence!

She took a deep breath, and launched into the delicate conversation.

'Is this because we kissed? Has one kiss turned you into some kind of cold robot? If so, that's ridiculous. It was a mistake so let's get past it. We've been friends for more than two years, Harry, and friends talk to one another. We can talk about this. Isn't that easier than carrying on as if we've broken some immutable law of nature? I mean, it was a nice kiss as kisses go, but it's not likely that we'll ever do it again.'

As the flippant words spun around the cabin of the vehicle, mingling with the radio's chatter and the wind that whirled outside, Grace felt her heart break.

But this was how it had to be. She didn't want Harry thinking the kiss meant any more to her than it had to him.

He glanced her way, his face still betraying nothing.

'*Do* we talk to one another?' he asked, delving so far back into Grace's conversation it took her a moment to remember she'd made the comment.

'Yes,' she said, although doubts were now popping up in her head.

They did talk, but about their work, their friends, the hospital, the town, the price of sugar cane—Harry's father being the owner of the local mill—the weather, and just about everything under the sun.

'Not about ourselves,' Harry said, still staring resolutely through the windscreen, although, given the debris flying through the air, that was a very good idea. 'Today's the first time I've heard you mention a father.'

'Everyone has one,' Grace said glibly, but the look Harry gave her told her flippancy wasn't going to work.

'OK, you're right. We don't talk much about ourselves,' Grace admitted, though she wasn't sure what this had to do with the kiss, or with Harry's mood. 'But talking's a two-way street, Harry. Talking—really talking—means sharing small parts of yourself with another person, and it's hard to do that if the other person isn't willing to share as well. Sharing that kind of talk leads to intimacy in a friendship and intimacy leaves people vulnerable. You treat everyone the same way probably because you don't want that intimacy—don't want anyone coming that close to you. The last thing in the world you'd want to seem is vulnerable.'

Harry glanced her way, frowned, then turned his attention back to the road, slowing down as the branch of a blue fig tree crashed onto the road right in front of them. He manoeuvred the car carefully around it.

'So you start the talking,' he finally said, totally ignoring her comments about his behaviour. 'Is it just because of your father you don't like weddings?'

It was the very last conversational gambit Grace had expected.

'Who said I don't like weddings?'

'You were so tense you could have snapped in half in there this afternoon.'

Because it *was* a wedding and I was sitting next to you, and it was hard not to indulge, for just a wee while, in a pointless daydream.

Grace was tempted to say it—to tell him of her feelings. The way the wind was blowing, literally, and sending tree limbs onto the road, they could both be killed any minute.

Would it be better or worse if Harry died knowing she loved him?

The thought of Harry dying made her heart squeeze into a tight little ball, while memories of the one time she *had* told a man she loved him made her cringe back into the seat.

She could still hear James's voice—his snide 'Love, Gracie? How quaint! What a sweet thing you are! Next you'll be telling me you're thinking of babies.'

Which she had been.

No wonder she could still feel the hurt...

'Well?' Harry persisted, and Grace had to think back to his question.

'It wasn't the wedding,' she managed to say, as Harry slammed on the brakes and his left arm shot out to stop her forward momentum.

'Thank heaven for traction control,' he muttered as the car skidded sideways towards the edge of the road then stopped before plunging off the side of the mountain. 'What was it, then?'

Grace shook her head.

'I can't believe we're having this conversation,' she said. 'Any minute now a tree's going to land across us and you're worried about why I was tense at the wedding.'

She paused, then added crossly, 'Anyway, this conversation isn't about me—it's about you. I didn't change from a friend to a frozen robot in the time it took to drive from town up the mountain.' She peered out through the windscreen. 'Why have we stopped?'

'I don't like the look of that tree.'

Harry pointed ahead and, as Grace followed the line of his finger, the huge forest red gum that had been leaning at a crazy angle across the road slid slowly downwards, the soaked soil on the mountainside releasing its tangle of roots so carefully it was only in the last few feet the massive trunk actually crashed to the ground.

'Oh!'

The nearest branches of the tree were right in front of the bonnet of Harry's vehicle, so close some of their smaller limbs were resting on it.

'We'll never clear it by hand. I'll radio for a car to come and get us on the other side, but we'll have to climb around the tree. For the moment, we'll just sit here until we're sure it's settled.'

Even as he said the words Harry regretted them. Of course they were safer in the vehicle than out there in the maelstrom of wind, rain and flying debris, but out there, talk would be impossible. In the car—in the dry warm cocoon it provided—even with the radio going, there was a false sense of—what?

He shuddered—Grace's word 'intimacy' seemed to fit.

What's more, there was no excuse to not talk…

He finished his call, telling base not to send someone to clear the tree as the conditions were too dangerous and the exercise pointless because the road was cut further up at the landslide. He glanced at Grace, who was still staring at the tree that hadn't collapsed on top of them, and he felt the stirring her blue dress had triggered earlier. She'd changed into her bulky but protective SES overalls, but hadn't removed the ribbon from her hair, so it now snaked through her wet curls, slightly askew so a bit of it crossed the top of her delicate pink ear.

He'd never looked at Grace's ears before, he realised as he reached over and used his forefinger to lift the ribbon from the ear then tease it gently out of her sodden hair. He had, of course, intended giving it back to her, but when she eyed the tatty wet object and muttered, 'What a fun way to end a wedding,' he decided she didn't want it, so he dropped it into his shirt pocket, did up the button and patted it into place.

He wasn't going to accept Grace's 'frozen robot' description, but he couldn't deny anger had been churning around inside him for the last few hours. Why *was* he so cranky?

Because he was worried, sure, but if he was honest with himself it was more than that. He could only suppose it was because Grace had added to his worries. From the moment she'd appeared at the accident site, he'd felt a new anxiety gnawing at his gut, and every time he saw her, each time wetter and paler than the time before, anxiety had taken another vicious bite.

That it was related to the kiss and the new attraction he felt towards her he had no doubt, but on a treacherous mountain road as a cyclone roared towards them and trees came crashing down, this was neither the time nor the place for introspection.

Or distraction.

Although maybe if he kissed her again, it would sort itself out. He could spend the waiting time kissing her, which would also make talking impossible. His body liked the idea, but his head knew that was the worst possible way to pass the time.

However appealing it might seem.

'You didn't answer about the kiss.'

Her statement startled him. There she was, still staring at the tree, yet picking up on some vibe he didn't know he was giving out.

But this was Grace—she deserved an honest answer.

'It was physical attraction, Grace,' he began, and waited to see if she'd turn towards him. Perhaps speak and save him the necessity of saying more.

She didn't, although she did glance his way momentarily.

'Strong physical attraction—we both felt it—but physical, that's all.'

Another glance, then all he got was her profile, although he fancied now she might be frowning, so he waited some more.

'And that's bad?' she finally queried.

'I believe it is. Well, not necessarily bad in a right and wrong sense, but dangerous, Grace. Misleading. Troublesome.' There, it had been said. Now they could get back to being friends.

Or as close to friends as they'd be able to get after his comments earlier.

CHAPTER FOUR

GRACE stared out through the windscreen at the fallen tree as she ran the explanation through her head, suspecting it might be Harry's way of saying that physical attraction was all he could feel for a woman these days. Putting it like that was less blunt that telling her he was still in love with his dead wife and always would be.

And although she'd always kind of suspected this, the confirmation of the idea caused Grace pain—physical pain, like a cramp around her heart.

The hateful, hurtful words, *you're not my wife*, took on a whole new meaning.

Perhaps she was wrong, and he wasn't saying that at all. One last gulp of hope remained in the balloon. Forgetting she was supposed to be distancing herself, she turned back towards him, determined to sort this out once and for all.

'Why is it dangerous? Misleading?'

Harry was staring at her, frowning slightly as if he wasn't certain who she was, and showed no sign of understanding her questions, let alone answering them.

'You must have a reason for believing it's bad,' she persisted.

Harry, who'd been thinking how pretty her eyes were and wondering why he'd never considered Grace's eyes before any more than he'd considered her ears, shrugged off the remark, although he suspected she wasn't going to let this go. But how could he explain the still bruised part of his heart that was Nikki? Explain the magnitude of their mistake?

'We should start walking.'

'No way!' She nodded towards the radio which had just advised them the car was forty-five minutes away. 'Even if it takes us half an hour to get over or around the tree, we'd still be waiting in the rain for fifteen minutes, and that's if the road's not blocked further down.'

He nodded, conceding her point, but said nothing, pretending fascination with the babble on the radio— trying to forget where physical attraction had led once before *and* trying to block out the insidious desire creeping through his body every time he looked at Grace.

He patted his pocket.

One more kiss won't hurt, his physical self tempted, but a glance at Grace, wet curls plastered to a face that was pinched with tiredness, told him that it would hurt.

If not him, then definitely her.

And he hated the idea of hurting Grace any more than he had already.

Hated it!

Another glance her way told him she was still waiting for an answer.

Would wait all night…

'It confuses things,' he said. 'I mean, look at us, good friends, and suddenly we're all hung up over a kiss.'

'We weren't exactly good friends when it happened,' she reminded him. 'And *I'm* not hung up over it.'

'Maybe not, but you're only pushing this kiss business because you don't want to talk about why you were so uptight at the wedding.' Good thinking, Harry, turn defence into attack. 'That, if you remember, Grace, was where this conversation started. With the fact that we don't really talk to each other. And now I know about your father, I would think you'd be as wary of physical attraction as I am. Or did he fall madly and totally in love with all four of his wives?'

It was a low blow, and he sensed she'd cringed a little from it, making him feel a bastard for hurting her. But it would be better this way—with the kiss passed off as the aberration he was sure it was and the two of them getting on with the friendship they'd always shared.

Not totally convinced by this seemingly sensible plan, he checked the weather, acknowledged an ETA call from the car coming to collect them, waited until the wail of the three hourly cyclone warning coming from the radio stopped, then pushed his companion a little further.

'Do you know what I know about you, Grace? Really know about you?' He didn't wait for her to answer, but held up two fingers. 'Two personal things—that's all. You hate being called Gracie, and you think you're too short.'

'I think I'm too short?' Grace repeated, confused by

that accusation and disturbed by the 'Gracie' echo of her own thoughts earlier. 'What makes you think I think I'm too short?'

He had the hide to smile at her! Smug smile of a man who thought he'd scored a point.

'Because of the way you throw yourself into things—especially the SES. You told me you joined the equivalent operation down there in Victoria the moment you were old enough—why? I bet it was because people had always seen you as small and cuddly and cute but in need of protection, and you had to prove to them and to yourself that you could hold your own both with bigger, taller women and with men. I see it every time we're on calls together and even when we're doing exercises—you have to go first and go highest, or deepest, or whatever. You're proving you're not only equal to other team members but better than most of them.'

'And you think that's because I'm short?' Grace demanded, hoping she sounded incredulous, not upset because he'd read her so well—although she'd got past proving her stuff a long time ago.

'I know it was, but now it's probably because you are the best—or one of the best—that you do the things you do.'

Conceding her point was definitely a low blow but, unable to refute this statement, she went back to the original bit of the 'short' conversation.

'You can add a third thing to what you know of me—I hate being thought cute!'

Harry smiled again, causing chaos in Grace's body—palpitations, tingling nerves, butterflies swarming in her stomach. Not good things to feel towards a man who'd more or less admitted he'd never love again. Not good things to feel when she was in her getting-over-him phase.

'You're especially cute when you're angry,' he teased, sounding like her friend Harry once again, although the palpitations persisted, accompanied by a twinge of sadness for what couldn't be.

Attack—that would be a good distraction for both her heart and her head.

'Well, I don't know how you can talk about always going highest or deepest—at least I don't take risks,' she told him. 'You're the one who plunges into situations the rest of us feel are too dangerous.'

'I'm not a volunteer like you guys. It's my job.'

No smile, and he'd turned away so all she could see was his profile. Hard to read, Harry's profile, although it was very nice to look at. Very well defined with its straight nose and black brow shadowing a deep-set eye. High cheekbones with shadows underneath, and lips—

She had to stop this! She had to push her feelings for Harry back where they belonged—deeply hidden in her heart.

For the moment.

Just till she got rid of them altogether.

Returning to the attack might help…

'Oh, yes? Like every policeman in Australia would have gone down in those shark-infested waters, with a storm raging, to rescue that diver?'

'Every policeman who can swim,' he said, smiling to lessen the lie in the ridiculous statement.

'Rubbish!' Grace dismissed both smile and lie with

a wave of her hand. 'If your guess—and I'm not admitting it's right, Harry—is that I went into the SES because I was short, then my guess is you do all this dangerous stuff because you don't give a damn about what happens to you. That's understandable to a certain extent, given the loss of your wife. Taking risks might have helped dull the pain at first but now it's become a habit.'

Sheesh! Was she really doing this? Talking to Harry about his wife, and his attraction to danger? The very subject he'd warned her off last night?

And how was he reacting now?

He'd turned away, the profile gone, and all she had was a good view of slightly over-long hair.

Silky hair—she'd felt it when her fingers had somehow made their way to the back of his head as they'd kissed.

Her fingers were remembering the slide of his hair against her skin when he turned back to face her.

Half smiling…

'I asked for that,' he said quietly, reaching out and touching her face, perhaps pushing a wet curl off her forehead. 'Saying that we never talked.'

Then he leaned towards her and very gently pressed a kiss against her lips.

'Time to move, my tall, brave SES friend. Where's your hard hat?'

The tender kiss and Harry's softly teasing voice caught at Grace's heart and made her vision blur for an instant. But Harry was right—they had to move, and she had to get her mind off kisses and tenderness and concentrate on getting around the tree.

She felt around her feet for the hard hat then re-membered she'd given it to the volunteer who'd climbed into the bus to tend that final passenger while others had cut her free. The helmet had a lamp on it that meant he'd been able to see what he'd been doing.

She explained this to Harry who made a huffing noise as if such an action had been stupid.

'Not that it matters now,' she told him. 'They never do much to keep off the rain.'

But Harry had other ideas, reaching behind him for the wide-brimmed felt hat issued to all police officers up here in the tropics and plonking it down on her head.

'There, it suits you,' he said, and she had to smile.

'Because it's so big it covers all my face?'

The hat had dropped to eyebrow level, but she could still see Harry's face, and caught the frown that replaced the smile he'd offered with the hat.

'That's another thing I know about you,' he said crossly. 'You're always putting yourself down. Not like some women do when they're looking for compliments, but it's as if you genuinely believe you're not smart, and pretty, and…'

Grace had her hand on the catch of the door, ready to open it and brave the wild weather outside, but Harry's pronouncement stopped her.

'And?' she asked, half wanting to know, half uncer-tain.

'And tonight in that blue thing you looked beautiful,' he said. 'Bloody beautiful!'

He was out the door before Grace could react. Actually, if he hadn't opened her door for her he could have been halfway to Crocodile Creek before she reacted, so lost was she in a warm little cloud of happiness.

Harry thought she'd looked beautiful…

Bloody beautiful…

Harry shut the car door, took Grace's hand and drew her close to his body. Since Grace had forced him to think about it, he'd realised his problem was physical attraction mixed with angry concern. The combination was so unsettling it was muddling both his mind and his body at a time when his brain needed to be crystal clear and all his senses needed to be on full alert.

On top of that, his inability to do anything about their current precarious situation—to protect Grace from this fury Nature was flinging at them—had his jaw clenched and his muscles knotted in frustration.

And his leg hurt…

He tried to tuck Grace closer as they followed the beam of light from his torch, clambering over the lesser boughs and branches, heads bent against the wind and rain. She was so slight—had she lost weight lately and he hadn't noticed?—she could blow away.

He gripped her more tightly.

'Harry!'

Had she said his name earlier that this time she pressed her lips against his ear and yelled it?

'What?'

'I think that way's clearer,' she yelled, pointing towards the base of the tree. 'There's a branch there we can use to climb onto the trunk, and even if we have to jump off the other side, it might be better than scrambling through the tangle of branches up this way.'

She was right and he should have worked it out himself, but the mess on the road was nothing to the mess in his head. He had to get past it—to rid his mind of all extraneous thoughts. Tonight, more than ever before, he'd need to be clear-headed in order to protect the people of his town.

She'd moved away though still held his hand, leading him in the direction she'd indicated, picking her way over the fallen branches. A sudden whistling noise made him look up and he dived forward, seizing Grace in a flying tackle, landing with her against the protective bulk of the huge treetrunk.

The branch that had whistled its warning crashed to the ground in front of them.

'This is ridiculous. I want you to go back and wait in the car,' he said, holding her—too tightly—in his arms, desperate to keep her safe.

'Are you going back to sit in the car?' she asked, snuggling up against his chest, which didn't help the mess in his head.

'Of course not. There's a cyclone coming. I have to get back to town.'

She reached up and patted his cheek.

'So do I,' she said softly. 'So maybe we'd better get moving again.'

'No thank-you kiss for saving your life?'

Oh, no! Had he really said that? What was wrong with him? The very last thing he needed to be doing was kissing Grace.

'I think kissing has caused enough problems tonight, don't you?' she replied, but the hand that was resting on his cheek moved and one fingertip traced the outline of his lips, reminding him of the heat the kiss had generated earlier—stirring the glowing coals of it back to life.

He stood up, still holding her, controlling breathing that was suddenly erratic, while looking around for any new source of danger. But though the wind still blew, it seemed relatively safe.

'I'm going to boost you up onto the trunk. Get over the top and into the shelter of it on the other side as quickly as you can.'

He lifted her—so light—and set her on the trunk, then heaved himself up, his leg objecting yet again to the rough treatment it was getting. Then he followed her as she dropped swiftly down to road level again. There were fewer branches to trip or slow them down on this side, so he took her hand again and hurried her along the road, sure the car would meet them before long, although driving through the storm had its own problems.

'Lights!'

Grace pointed as she yelled the word at Harry. Even if he didn't hear her, he'd surely see the lights. She couldn't wait to get to the car, not because the wind and rain and flying leaves and branches bothered her unduly but to get away from Harry—out of touching distance, where it was impossible to make sense of all that had happened during the course of this weird evening.

The thought that Harry might be physically attracted to her had filled her with joy, but his evident distrust of such attraction could only mean he still had feelings for his wife. In his mind, physical attraction to another woman must seem like betrayal—a form of infidelity—although Nikki had been dead for nearly three years.

Then there was the question of whether they were still friends.

And her determination to move on from Harry—now made harder than ever because of the kiss.

Grace sighed. If she wanted a husband and family, she *had* to move on. She may have looked beautiful in her blue dress earlier today, but what chance did she have against the memory of a woman who'd not only been tall and slim and elegant, but a former local beauty queen—the Millennium Miss Caneland—and a popular television personality?

Even when she was dying, Nikki Blake had been beautiful. Grace had seen enough photos of her to know that much.

And nice with it, according to the staff who'd nursed her.

Grace sighed again.

'Not right. The lights aren't getting closer.'

She caught the end of Harry's sentence and peered ahead through the worsening deluge. Not only weren't the lights moving, but they appeared to be pointing upwards.

'He's slid off the road.'

Harry's words confirmed her thoughts and she broke into a jog, running behind him as he dropped her hand and raced towards the lights.

Hairpin bends around the mountain—they rounded one, then two, and were on the outward curve of a third when they saw the vehicle, which had come to rest against a pillar-shaped rock, its headlights pointing uselessly into the blackness of the forest.

'Stay here,' Harry ordered, but Grace was already picking her way carefully down the slope, testing each foothold before shifting her weight.

The torch beam cut through the useless illumination provided by the vehicle's headlights, but revealed nothing more than a cloud of white behind the wind-screen. The air bags had obviously worked.

Then, as the torch beam played across the vehicle, Grace saw a movement, a hand, pushing at the cloud of white, fighting against it.

'It's Troy!'

Harry's voice held all the anxiety and pain she knew he'd feel about this, the youngest of the men on his staff.

'Sit still,' he yelled, scrambling faster down the slope, cursing his bad leg, and unheeding of the danger to himself as he plummeted towards the young policeman. 'The less you move, the less risk there is of the vehicle moving.'

Grace followed more cautiously, aware, as Harry was, that Troy wouldn't hear the warnings over the wind and through windows wound up tightly against the weather.

Harry reached the car, more careful now, not touching it—not touching anything—but circling, mo-tioning with both hands for Troy, whose face was now visible, to be still. Grace stopped a little further up the hill, then turned to look back the way they'd come.

'Would you trust that red gum to hold the car if we wind the winch cable around it?'

She pointed towards a tree not unlike the one that

had fallen close to them earlier, but this one was on the far side of the road.

'We'll have to,' Harry said. 'For a start, we'll just use it to anchor the vehicle while we get Troy out. I won't risk using the winch with him in the cabin. You stay clear of everything while I take the cable up to the tree.'

He made his way to the front of the vehicle where the winch was sited and bent to release the cable.

Grace watched the careful way he touched the winch and understood his caution. The vehicle might seem secure enough, resting as it was against a massive rock, but with all the rain they'd had, the rock could have been undermined and any change in the dynamics of the vehicle could send it and Troy plummeting into the gully.

'Damn! I can't get in the back to get a bag,' Harry muttered, looking helplessly around then focussing on Grace. 'I don't suppose you're wearing something—no, of course you're not. It'll have to be my jacket.'

He handed the hook of the winch cable to Grace to hold and for the first time she realised he was still in his dinner suit. The bow-tie was gone but, yes, that was definitely a filthy, sodden dinner jacket he was removing.

'What do you need it for?' Grace asked as he took the cable hook from her and turned towards the road.

He looked back at her and smiled.

'To wrap around the tree. We all keep bags in the back of our vehicles to use as tree protection but as I can't get at a bag, the jacket will have to do. If there's no protection the steel cable can ringbark the tree and possibly kill it.'

Grace shook her head. Here they were in the rain-forest, with gale-force winds and torrential rain whipping the vegetation to ribbons, and Harry was protecting a gum tree?

She watched him clamber and limp his way back up to the road, seeing the way his wet shirt clung to his skin, defining the muscles and bones as well as if he'd been naked.

She shut her eyes, trying to blot images of a naked Harry from her mind, then turned back to Troy, using her hands as Harry had, to motion him to stillness, smiling encouragement. And something worked because although all his instincts must be screaming at him to escape the confines of the vehicle, he stayed where he was—statue still.

'I'll just hook this up—doubling the cable back to the vehicle halves the weight on the winch, although the vehicle's only a couple of tons and the winch's weight capacity is five tons.' Harry explained, returning with the hook end of the cable, which he attached to a towing point at the front of the vehicle. 'Now, I'll take up any slack in the cable then get in the cab to check the lad.'

'*I'll* get in the cab to check him,' Grace said. 'And don't bother arguing because you know it makes sense. I weigh half as much as you do so, like with the cable, we're halving the risk of the vehicle moving.'

Even in the torchlight she saw Harry's lips tighten, going white with the pressure of not arguing, but in the end he gave a nod.

This wasn't anything to do with the new physical at-traction, Harry assured himself as he very carefully opened the passenger door of the cambered vehicle—

the door not jammed against the rock. His anxiety was for Grace, his friend.

'You OK?' he asked, peering through the maze of white towards the young constable.

'I think I've hurt my leg.'

Troy's voice wavered slightly and Harry understood. Barely more than a kid, he'd had to drive out through the wind and rain and flying missiles, then the car had skidded and he'd thought he'd had it.

'Grace will check you out,' Harry told him, turning towards Grace so he could help her into the cabin.

Beneath his wide-brimmed hat, her face was pale and streaked with dirt, and the embattled smile she gave him tweaked at something in his heart.

Concern, that's what it was. The same concern that was making his stomach knot as she slid across the seat, cutting at the air bags with the penknife off her belt, talking all the time to Troy about where he hurt and how he felt.

'There'll be a torch snapped in grips underneath the dash,' he told Grace when she'd collapsed the air bags and pulled them out of the way.

'Thanks!'

She found the torch and turned it on, setting it down so its light shone on her patient. Then, as her small but capable hands slid across Troy's head, feeling for any evident damage, Harry remembered this was only the beginning of the salvage operation. Unless they wanted to walk the forty-odd kilometres back to Crocodile Creek, he had to get this vehicle back up onto the road.

He prowled around it, checking the tyres—all intact—and damage to the body that might inhibit movement of the wheels. The mudguard, which had taken the brunt of the collision with the rock, was pushed in, but he found a strong branch and levered it off the rubber of the tyre. Everything else looked OK, which wasn't surprising as his reading of the accident had the vehicle going into a slow slide, first across the road, then down the slope to where it had come to rest against the rock.

'Where do you keep the first-aid kit in these new vehicles?' Grace called to him, and he turned to see she'd clambered over the back of the front seat and was now searching around behind the back seats.

'It should be strapped against the back of that seat you're on,' he told her, managing to answer although his lungs didn't want to breathe while she was moving in the cabin.

'Got it. I think Troy's right leg might be broken. I'll give him a painkiller before I try to move him, then splint it as best I can.'

She turned back to her patient, the small medical kit already open on her lap.

'Actually, Troy, it might be best if you fainted when we move you. That way you mightn't feel the pain so much.'

The lad grinned at Grace and Harry shook his head. They were like two kids playing doctors, seemingly unaware that a twisted metal cable was all that held them from the very real possibility of death.

'Do we really need to get him out?'

Grace had skidded across the seat to speak quietly to Harry, while Troy's eyelids were closing, no doubt in response to the drug she'd given him.

'I don't want to try winching it with anyone inside,' Harry told her once again. 'In ordinary circumstances it's better for have someone steering, but not in this situation where we don't know if the anchoring tree will hold the weight. The winch will pull the front around this way, then drag the vehicle up the slope.'

'We hope,' Grace said, and for the first time since their adventure together had begun she sounded tired.

'The cable's holding—let me in there!' Harry said, his stomach knotting with more anxiety.

'No, I'll manage and I need you there to help Troy out and lift him down to the ground. Would there be something in the back we can wrap him in? He's already shocky from the accident and his leg. I don't want that getting worse.'

Harry pictured the gear they all carried in the back of the big police vehicles.

'There'll be a small waterproof tarp folded in the pocket behind the driver's seat and a space blanket in a pouch beside it. Get them both out and we'll wrap him in the space blanket then the tarp. It will make moving him easier as well.'

Grace found them both and wriggled across the seat to drop them out the door to Harry, then, satisfied the painkiller had had time to work, she turned her attention back to her patient.

Her first examination of him had told her he was holding up well. His pulse and breathing were steady, his pupils responding evenly to light, and he was able to move all his limbs so the front and side air bags seemed to have done their jobs, protecting his head and holding his body firmly in the seat belt so his spine wasn't compromised.

But even with a painkiller circulating in his blood and blocking messages to and from his brain, he was going to be in agony when he moved his leg.

'Troy, I need to get you over onto this passenger seat before we can get you out. The best way I can see to do it would be for you to lie sideways across the centre console so your head and shoulders are on the passenger seat behind me, then if you can bring your good leg up onto your seat and use it to help you inch your way towards the door until your butt's on this side. Can you do that?'

Troy looked at her, his eyes glazed by the medication, but he nodded and turned so he could wiggle across the seat. His groan as he moved confirmed her thoughts, but she had to get him out of the vehicle before she could splint his leg and stabilise him properly.

She was squatting in the footwell on the passenger side, her body canted across the gear lever as she reached out to take a firm grip on his injured leg. She had to get it up onto the seat of the car before she could examine the damage and was concentrating on doing this is carefully as possible, trying not to hurt him, when the vehicle moved.

Troy let out a yelp, and Harry roared, 'Keep still!'

'As if I needed to be told that!' Grace muttered to herself, frozen in place with Troy's calf held gingerly in her hands.

'It's my weight coming onto this side,' Troy said.

But it was Harry's 'I need to get you both out now!' that caught Grace's attention.

She couldn't see anything from where she was so she continued with her job, lifting Troy's injured leg up onto the seat.

He gave a whistling sigh then slumped against the seat, the pain making him pass out.

Swelling around his ankle suggested the problem was there, or at the base of his tib and fib, but there was no time to do anything but get him out, preferably while he was still unconscious.

'How are we going to do this?' she called to Harry, who now had the door propped or tied open in some way.

'You push his shoulders down towards me, and I'll ease him out. Do what you can to protect his leg as we move him.'

Back in the footwell on the passenger side, she eased Troy's body around so his shoulders slid out the door. Harry's hands caught him, then lifted him as Grace grasped the injured limb to lift it over the centre console and gently out the door.

Harry cradled the young man in his arms, holding him as easily as she'd have held a baby, then he knelt and rested his burden on the spread-out covers on the ground, so carefully Grace shook her head in wonder at his gentle strength.

'The space blanket's a bit wet but it will still keep his body warmth in,' he said, wrapping first it and then the tarp around Troy's upper body, leaving his legs un-wrapped so Grace could see to his injury.

Again using her knife, she cut through the leather of

his boot, wanting to ease the constriction on his blood vessels that the swelling would be causing.

'Does he need this to order a new pair?' she asked Harry, tossing the wrecked boot to one side, cutting off Troy's sock now so she could put a half-splint around his foot to hold it steady while allowing for more swelling.

The police car's first-aid kit didn't run to splints, but there were plenty of sticks which she could pad with torn strips of sock before binding them into place around his foot and ankle.

Harry watched her work—small, capable hands moving so steadily she might have been in A and E, not on a dangerous, slippery slope with wind and rain raging about her.

She was good!

'OK?'

Had she said something that he'd missed while thinking about her, that now she was standing beside him, waiting for a response?

'He's done?'

Harry looked down at the young policeman who was now fully wrapped in the space blanket and tarp.

'We just need to get him up the hill,' Grace said, nodding up the slope. 'I'll take his legs.'

For a moment Harry considered arguing but although he'd been able to lift Troy free, he knew he couldn't carry him all the way up the slippery hill when he was healthy, let alone with a bung leg. Between them they lifted the injured man and carried him up the slope, slipping and sliding, Troy groaning from time to time, but eventually they had him safely on the road.

Grace took off Harry's hat and placed it, carefully tilted, on Troy's head to keep the worst of the rain from his face, then she watched as Harry made his way back down the slope and, using a hand-held remote control, started the winch.

She heard the winch motor whirr and held her breath then, oh, so slowly, the front of the big police vehicle swung around and, with wheels churning the surface of the slope to mud, it began to move, inch by inch, towards the tree that held its weight.

Harry had placed Troy well away from where the car would reach the road, and out of danger should the tree fall, but still Grace felt her nerves tighten, fear for all of them should the tree come down, or the vehicle not make the road, clutching at her stomach.

It was nearly up, front wheels on the verge, the winch whining complaints all the way, when the back wheels skidded, sending a final flurry of slush into the air before ploughing forward onto the bitumen.

'You did it!' Grace yelled, abandoning her patient to jump up in the air in excitement. She'd have hugged Harry if their earlier conversation hadn't suggested even friendly hugs should be avoided. 'You got it up!'

'But will it go?'

Harry's question tempered her delight, but she sensed satisfaction in his voice and knew he was fairly confident the vehicle would be drivable. He was unhooking the towing cable, then using the winch to wind it up, while Grace walked over to the tree to retrieve his dinner jacket.

'Beyond repair?' Harry asked, seeing the muddy, crumpled garment in her hands.

'We'll see,' she said, clutching the jacket to her chest, holding onto something that was Harry's, barely restraining an urge to sniff at it in the hope of picking up something of his scent.

'You're so tired you've gone loopy!' she muttered to herself, returning to her patient, who was peering out from underneath the hat, no doubt wondering if there was any chance he could be moved out of the rain.

Harry started the car then drove slowly towards them, checking the vehicle was safe to drive. He stopped beside Troy and Grace, leaping out to open the back door and lift Troy inside.

'See if you can strap him in there so he's comfortable,' he said to Grace, who scrambled in beside her patient. 'Then you hop in the front and put on your seat belt. We don't want any more patients delivered to the hospital today.'

Grace obeyed, making Troy as comfortable as she could, checking his pulse again before abandoning him to climb over into the front seat and strap on her seat belt.

'OK?' Harry turned towards her as he asked, and the smile he offered was so kind Grace felt tears prickle behind her eyelids. She knew it was relief that they were all safe, and tiredness as it had been a very long day, but try as she may she couldn't answer him, making do with a very watery smile instead.

She was exhausted, Harry realised, remembering something she'd said that morning when they'd been called out to an accident at Wygera—something about just coming off night duty.

'When did you last sleep?' he demanded, anxiety making his voice more abrupt than he'd intended.

But Grace didn't answer. She was already asleep.

At least he'd got everyone off the mountain...

'Scruffy!'

Max slid and scrambled down the hill, stumbling over rocks, ducking around the ferns, yelling until he thought his chest would burst.

The bus had been on its side, that's all he remembered. The bus being on its side and no windows where the windows should have been.

No Scruffy either.

His dog was gone.

'Scruffy! Come on, boy. Scruffy!'

He listened for the yelp that Scruffy always gave in answer to his name, but how to hear a small dog's yelp when the wind was howling and stuff was crashing in the bush all around him?

'Scruffy!'

CHAPTER FIVE

HARRY drove carefully down the road, one hand fiddling with the radio, which seemed to be the only thing not working in the vehicle. Had a wire come loose? He twirled knobs and banged his hand against it, but couldn't pick up even a burst of static.

No distraction there…

He checked the rear-view mirror. Troy appeared to be asleep as well. So he looked back at Grace, at her pale face and almost translucent eyelids, at the shadows under her eyes and the spread of freckles now dark against her skin.

Grace!

He shook his head, unable to deny the attraction that still stirred within his body.

What was happening to him? Why had his body chosen this of all times to remind him of his physical needs?

And chosen Grace of all women?

He guessed a psychologist would tell him it was because the grieving process was finally over, but he knew what had kept him celibate since Nikki's death had been as much guilt as grief. Guilt for the pain he'd caused her. Yes, there'd been grief as well, grief that someone as young and lovely as Nikki should have to die. Grief for the child he'd lost. And grief for the friendship he'd damaged somewhere along the way in his relationship with Nikki.

He looked at Grace, knowing a similar close friendship was at risk here.

Grace! Every now and then, in the past, he'd caught a fleeting glimpse of another Grace behind the laughing, bubbly exterior most people saw—a glimpse of a Grace that disturbed him in some way.

Tonight, learning about her father—thinking about a small child flying all the way from Ireland to Australia in search of the love she hadn't found—he'd found a clue to the hidden Grace and understood a little of the pain and tears behind the laughter.

So now, more than ever, he didn't want to hurt her...

'Did I sleep?'

Grace peered blearily around her. They were in the emergency entrance at the hospital and, outside the car, Harry was holding the rear door while a couple of orderlies lifted Troy onto a stretcher.

'Like a log,' Harry told her, his smile lifting the lines tiredness had drawn on his face.

'No, stay right where you are,' he added, as she began to unbuckle her seat belt. 'I'm taking you home. Quite apart from the fact you're exhausted, you're so filthy you're the last thing anyone would want in a hospital.'

'You're not so sprucy clean yourself,' Grace retorted,

taking in the mud streaks on the wet shirt that clung to Harry's chest.

Then, remembering, she clutched his dinner jacket more tightly.

Pathetic, that's what she was, but the filthy, ragged garment in her hands had become some kind of talisman.

Though it would hardly have the power to ward off a cyclone.

'Willie?' she asked, looking beyond the well-lit area to where the wind still lashed the trees and threw rain horizontally against the building.

'Definitely heading our way.' Harry watched the orderlies wheel Troy towards the hospital, obviously torn between wanting to follow and getting Grace home. 'We're down to hourly warnings.'

'Then I've got work to do,' Grace said, unbuckling her seat belt once again. 'You go with Troy, I'll grab a hospital car, go home and change, then see what's happening on the evacuation front. I assume the SES crews started with the nursing home down by the river, so most of those people should be in the civic centre hall by now. I'll get the list and organise for all the others to be collected or chivvied into shifting under their own steam.'

She'd opened the car door while she'd proposed this eminently sensible plan, but Harry took the door from her grasp, used one firm hand to push her back into the seat and shut the door again.

'I'll take you home,' he repeated. 'Two minutes to see someone's attending to Troy and I'll be right back. We need to do the individual evacuations on our list together. We discussed this in the contingency meetings. You'll need police presence to get some of those stubborn elderly die-hards in the most flimsy of old houses to move.'

Grace acknowledged his point with a pathetically weak smile. Battling wind and rain and an approaching cyclone was bad enough, but battling all the conflicting emotions the evening had stirred up at the same time was making the job doubly—no, a hundred times—more difficult.

Harry followed Troy's stretcher into A and E, where the scene resembled something from the film set of a disaster movie.

Only this wasn't a movie, it was real.

'How's it going?' he asked Charles, who had rolled towards him as Troy was taken into a treatment cubicle.

'It looks worse than it is. I think we've got things under control, although we've some badly injured people here in the hospital. There's one young woman with head injuries. Thank heavens Alistair—you know Alistair? Gina's cousin?—was here. He's a neurosurgeon with skills far beyond anyone we have on staff. He's put her into an induced coma for the moment— who knows how she'll wake up? We lost one young girl, and that last patient…' Charles paused and shook his head. 'She died before she got here.'

He seemed to have aged, but Harry understood that—he felt about a hundred years old himself.

'How's everything out there? Did you get everyone off the mountain?'

Harry nodded then looked around again, looking ahead, not thinking back. He'd done enough of that lately.

'You've obviously cleared the walking wounded. Where are they?'

'If they weren't locals with homes to go to, they were sent to the civic centre hall. Volunteers there are providing food and hot drinks.'

Charles paused then added, 'Actually, if you're going that way and I'm sure you will be some time, you might take the belongings we haven't matched to patients with you and see if you can find owners for them at the hall. The gear's in Reception.'

Someone called to Charles, who wheeled away, while Harry strode through to Reception, aware he'd been longer than the two minutes he'd promised Grace. Perhaps she'd fallen asleep again.

Wet, squashed, some muddy, the belongings rescued from the bus formed a sorry-looking heap on the floor in one corner of the usually immaculate reception area. How was he going to ferry this lot out to the car? He'd walked through from the corridor, thinking about the belongings, and now saw the two people who stood beside it.

Georgie Turner and Alistair—the doctor Charles had mentioned. They would have been working flat out since the casualties had begun coming in, but they weren't thinking medicine now. Georgie was staring down at the small, muddy backpack in her hands. She'd emptied it—a pathetic bundle of child's clothing and a ragged teddy bear had tumbled out and were lying at her feet.

While he watched, she knelt and lifted the teddy bear. The face she raised to him was terror-stricken.

'Max was on that bus,' she whispered.

'Your Max?'

Harry found himself staring helplessly at her. Georgie's beloved Max—hell's teeth, they all loved Max.

'Harry, have you found any kids?' Georgie demanded. And then the remaining colour drained out of her face. 'He's not…he's not one of the bodies, is he? Oh, God, please…'

'He's not,' Harry said, crossing swiftly to her, kneeling and gripping her hands. 'Georgie, I've been up there. We searched the surrounding area. We found no kids.'

'His dad… Ron's on the run. They might both…'

'I know Ron, Georgie. He wasn't on the bus.'

'But he might be hiding. He might—'

'Georgie, any person in that bus would be far too battered to be thinking about hiding. And the wind's unbelievable. Ron might be afraid of jail but there are worse things than jail, and staying out in the rainforest tonight would be one of them.'

'But Max is definitely there,' Georgie faltered. She looked up at Harry. 'He is,' she said dully, hugging the bear tighter. 'This is Spike. Max has just stopped carrying Spike round but Spike's never far from him.'

Behind them the phone rang, but the pile of child-size clothes on the floor reminded Harry of something.

'There's a shoe,' he told her, looking through the mass of wet belongings and not finding it. 'I'll just ask someone.'

He left the reception area, remembering the bridesmaid, Hannah, had found the shoe. Where was it now? He tracked it down at the desk of the children's ward.

The shoe was small and very muddy, with an orange

fish painted on it, the eye of the fish camouflaging a small hole.

Harry held it in his hand and hurried back to Georgie, showing her the shoe then seeing a quick shake of her head.

'That's not Max's.'

Her dismissal of it was so definite, Harry shoved the shoe into his pocket to think about later.

'We've got to go back out there,' Georgie added.

Images of young Max, a kid who'd had enough problems in his life thanks to his wastrel, drug-running father, alone in the bush, maybe injured, definitely wet, and probably terrified, flashed through Harry's mind. His gut knotted as he realised the impossibility of doing what she'd suggested.

'There's a tree across the road—we can't get through. I'd go myself and walk in, Georgie, but I can't leave town right now.'

He could feel her anguish—felt his own tearing him apart—but his duty had to be to the town, not to one small boy lost in the bush while a cyclone ripped the forest to shreds above his head.

'Of course you can't, go but I can. I'm going out there now.'

He saw the determination in her eyes, but could he stop her?

He had to try...

'Georgie, there's a cyclone hitting within hours. There's no way I can let you go, even if you could get through, which you can't. The tree's crashed down across the road not far from the landslide. We were lucky to get the last of the injured out.'

'I'll take my dirt bike,' she snapped. She tried to shove Harry aside but he wouldn't move.

Harry ignored the fists beating at his chest, trying desperately to think through this dilemma. Georgie could throw her bikes around as competently as she wore the four-inch heels she fancied as her footwear. She'd be wearing a helmet—

As if that would help!

'Georgie, he might not even be out there. You said yourself it's not his shoe.'

'Then there are two kids. Let me past.'

Georgie shoved at him but Harry held her, and made one last attempt to persuade her not to go.

'We've got no proof he's there. It's suicide.'

'We do have proof,' Alistair said from behind them. 'We've had confirmation Max was on the bus. Suicide or not, there's a child's life at stake. I'll go with her.'

Harry's mind processed what he knew of Alistair. Gina's cousin—Harry had met him at a fire party on the beach some months ago when the American had come to visit Gina—or more to check out Gina's fiancé Cal, the locals had thought.

Stuffed shirt had been Harry's immediate reaction.

Stuffed shirt who could ride a bike?

The pushing stopped. Georgie whirled to face Alistair, her face a mixture of anguish and fear. 'You can't.'

'Don't you start saying can't,' Alistair said. 'Harry, the tree's blocking the road, right? Who else in town has a dirt bike?'

'I've got one,' Harry told him, thinking it through. If Max *was* out there…

Maybe he had no choice but to let them go. 'It's in the shed, Georgie, fuelled up, key above the door. And be careful, keep in mind at all times that there are open mineshafts on that mountain.'

But Georgie wasn't listening. She was staring at Alistair.

'You really can ride?'

'I can ride.'

'You'd better not hold me back,' she snapped.

'Stop arguing and get going—you don't have long,' Harry told them. 'You've got a radio, Georg? Of course not. Here, take mine and I'll pick up a spare at the station. Your cellphone might or might not work. And take a torch, it's black as pitch out there. Rev your bikes, he might hear the noise.'

Harry watched them go then pulled the shoe out of his pocket, grasping it in his hand, feeling how small and insubstantial it was.

Were there two children lost in the bush?

Surely not.

But his heart clenched with worry, while his hands fondled the little painted shoe. Georgie had said it was too small for Max. Max was seven, so the shoe would fit…

A two-and-a-half-year-old?

Harry shook his head. Why did thoughts like that creep up on him at the most inopportune times?

And wasn't he over thinking back?

He tucked the shoe back into his pocket, gathered up a bundle of backpacks and suitcases and headed out to his vehicle, thanking someone who'd come out from behind the reception desk and offered to help carry things.

It wasn't until he'd packed them into the back of the big vehicle that he realised he'd lost his passenger.

'If you're looking for Grace, she went into A and E,' a nurse standing outside in the wind and rain, trying hard to smoke a cigarette, told him.

Harry was about to walk back inside when Grace emerged from the side door, head bowed and shoulders bent, looking so tired and defeated Harry hurried towards her, anxiety again gnawing at his intestines.

He reached her side and put his arms around her, pulling her into an embrace, holding her tightly as the wind and rain swirled around them.

'What's happened?' he asked as she burrowed her head into his chest as if trying to escape herself.

'She died.' The whispered words failed to register for a moment, then Grace lifted her head and looked up into his face. 'Our woman, Harry. The last one out of the bus. I've just seen Mike. She died before they reached the hospital. Massive brain injuries, nothing anyone could do.'

'Oh, Grace!' he said, and rocked her in his arms, knowing exhaustion was adding to the regret and hurt of the woman's death. He'd felt the same extreme reaction when Charles had given him that news.

'She had a boyfriend on the bus,' Grace continued. 'He was seated with her and got out uninjured, but she had to use the bathroom and was in there when it happened. They're from Germany and now he has to phone her parents.'

'I'll do that, it's my job,' Harry said, but Grace shook her head.

'Charles is phoning now—he speaks German so

he'll support the boy. But fancy someone phoning, Harry, to say your daughter's dead.'

She began to shiver and Harry led her to the car, helping her in, wanting to get her home and dry—and safe.

Safe? Where was safe tonight? Nowhere in Crocodile Creek, that was for sure.

Grace fell asleep again on the short drive to her cottage and this time, when he stopped the car, Harry sat and looked at her for a minute. He had the list and could do the evacuations himself, although that would be pretty stupid as he was likely to be needed other places or would be taking calls that would distract him.

And on top of that, she'd be furious.

He sighed, reached out to push a wet curl off her temple, then got out of the car, walked, with difficulty as the wind was far stronger here on the coast, around the bonnet, then carefully opened the passenger door, slipping his hand inside to hold Grace's weight so she didn't slide out.

Her lips opened in a small mew of protest at this disruption, but she didn't push him away so he reached across her and undid the catch on her seat belt, conscious all the time of the softness of her body and the steady rise and fall of her breasts.

She stirred again as he lifted her out, then she rested her head against his shoulder and drifted back to sleep.

But once inside he had to wake her—had to get her out of her sodden garments for a start.

'Grace!'

He said her name so softly he was surprised when she opened her eyes immediately. Was it her nursing training kicking in that she could come so instantly awake?

And frowning.

'Harry? Oh, damn, I fell asleep again. You should have woken me. You've carried more than your share of people tonight, and your leg must be killing you.'

'You don't weigh much. I'll set you down and as you still have power, I'll put the kettle on. I want you to get dry, have a hot drink then gather some things together for yourself. I'll drop you at the civic centre and you can sleep for a couple of hours.'

He eased her onto her feet just inside the door of her cottage.

'Sleep?' She looked so astounded he had to smile.

'What you've been doing in the car. Remember sleep?'

The feeble joke fell flat.

'I can't sleep now!' she muttered at him, then added a glare for good measure. 'Unless you're going to sleep as well,' she dared him. 'Then I might consider it.'

'You know I can't—not right now—but I'll be only too happy to grab a nap whenever I can. You should be, too, and now's as good a time as any.'

'So you can run around on your own, doing all the evacuations I'm supposed to be doing, fielding phone calls and giving orders and generally doing your super-hero thing. Well, not on my watch,' she finished, her usually soft pink lips set in a mutinous line.

He was about to deny the superhero accusation when he realised that was exactly what she wanted. She was turning the argument back on him.

'Well, fine,' he grumbled. 'But you're not going anywhere until you've had a hot drink.'

He stalked towards her kitchen.

Joe had obviously remembered the cyclone preparations from his time working in the town because the windows were all taped with broad adhesive tape, and a note on the kitchen table told them he'd taken Christina to the hospital because he was working there and hadn't wanted to leave her at the cottage on her own.

'Also large as she is,' he'd added, 'she swears she can still be useful.'

Harry filled the kettle, banging it against the tap because his frustration with Grace's behaviour still simmered.

'Stubborn woman!' he muttered to himself, finding the instant coffee and spooning a generous amount into two cups, adding an equal amount of sugar. It wasn't sleep but maybe a caffeine and sugar boost would help them tackle what still lay ahead of them this night.

Still grumpy, though not certain if it was because of Grace's refusal to obey his orders or her repetition of the superhero crack, he was carrying the filled cups and some biscuits he'd found in the pantry through to the living room when a small mumble of frustration made him turn. Grace was slumped on the sofa. She had managed to remove her boots but was now fumbling with the press studs that held her overalls together down the front.

Grumpiness was swallowed by concern so strong he felt shaken by the power of it.

'Here, let me,' Harry said, setting down the coffee and stepping towards her, telling her at the same time about the note and the preparations Joe had made, hoping the conversation might mask the trembling of his fingers.

He undid the studs then the Velcro strips and eased the heavy, wet fabric off Grace's shoulders. His voice— in the midst of explaining that Joe had left the water bottles, bedding, radio and batteries in the bathroom— faltered and his fingers shook a little more as he saw the swell of Grace's breasts, clad only in some scraps of dark blue lace—the colour making her ivory skin seem even paler.

Reminding himself that this was Grace, his friend, he helped her stand so he could drag the clammy, all-concealing garment off her body, trying desperately to ignore his body's reaction to the matching scrap of blue lace lower down, and the surprisingly shapely legs the stripping off of the garment revealed.

'You'll have to do the rest yourself,' he told her, his voice coming out as a throaty kind of growl.

'I had better,' she said, a teasing smile illuminating her tired face. 'Although,' she added wistfully, 'I'm not so certain physical attraction is all bad.'

'Right now any distraction at all is bad, Grace, and you know it. Now, scat, and take your coffee with you. Get into the shower and into some dry clothes—I'll slip home and change, check that everything's organised at the station and come back for you in ten or fifteen minutes.'

Getting away from her—doing things that needed doing—would surely distract him from...

From what?

He couldn't find an answer, and she didn't scat. She just stood there for a few seconds with her blue lace and white skin and exhausted face, seemingly about to say something, then she shook her head and turned away, revealing the fact that the blue lace was a thong so the pert roundness of her butt had him almost agreeing that physical attraction couldn't be all bad.

Except that he knew it was…

Grace stepped over the pile of emergency supplies Joe had deposited in her bathroom, and reached in to turn the shower on. She stripped off the sexy underwear she'd bought to go with the dress, sighing as she did so. She may as well have been wearing a nursing bra and bloomers for all the effect it had had on Harry. Although if she'd been too tired to argue as he'd stripped off her gear, he'd probably been too tired to think about attraction.

She showered, cringing as noises from above suggested half the forest was landing on the roof. Joe had been right to put the emergency gear in here—bathrooms were usually the safest room in the house, but if the roof blew off, or if a large branch caused damage, anyone sheltering in the bathroom would still get very wet.

'Better wet than dead,' she reminded herself, and a wave of sadness for a woman she didn't know engulfed her so suddenly she had to rest her head against the wall of the shower for a few minutes, hoping the hot water would sluice away the pain for those they hadn't saved.

Another crashing noise outside reminded her she had work to do, so she turned off the shower, dried herself and dressed hurriedly, pulling on a light pair of cargo pants with a multitude of pockets, and a T-shirt. Both would eventually be soaked even underneath a heavy raincoat but at least they'd dry faster when she was indoors. Boots next—only an idiot would be outside on a night like this without solid boots.

They were wet and didn't want to go on, and within minutes her dry socks had absorbed water from them. She shrugged off the discomfort, knowing it would soon be forgotten once she was involved in her work.

She unhooked her two-way radio and pocket knife from her belt and tucked them into the big pockets on her trousers, then added some spare batteries for the radio to another pocket. In the kitchen she found a packet of health bars and put four and a small bottle of water into the pockets down near her knees. Finally the list, carefully sealed inside a waterproof plastic bag, completed her preparations. She had another hard hat from her days in Victoria, and with that on her head and her bright yellow rain jacket around her shoulders, she headed out to the veranda to wait for Harry.

She'd taken down the hanging baskets from their hooks beneath the veranda roof before she'd dressed for the wedding, but although she'd packed them under other plants in the garden, one look at the already stripped stems told her how damaged they were going to get.

'Plants are replaceable,' she reminded herself, leaning against the wall as all the veranda chairs were stacked inside, but now, as she waited, her mind turned to Harry. Had it been the sense of imminent danger that had prompted them to speak of things that had always been unsaid between them?

She had no doubt that her friendship with Harry had developed, in part, because she *hadn't* been on the staff at the hospital when Nikki had died. Harry was the kind of man who would have shunned the sympathy on offer from all those who knew him—the kind of man who'd have pulled away from friends to work his grief out on his own.

But everyone needed someone and Grace had filled the void, providing a friendship not linked to either of their pasts and not going beyond the bounds of good but casual acquaintances.

If anything, since her discovery that she loved Harry, she'd pulled further back from anything approaching intimacy, so they'd laughed and joked and shared coffee and discussed ideas connected with the bits of their lives that touched—work and the SES.

She was still mulling over the shift in their relationship—if one kiss and some personal conversation could be called a shift—when Harry pulled into the drive. Pleased to be diverted from thoughts that were going nowhere—she was putting Harry out of her life, remember—she dashed towards the car, ducking as a plastic chair went flying by.

'Some stupid person hasn't tied down his outside furniture,' Harry muttered as she did up her seat belt.

'It looked like one of the chairs from beside the pool at the doctors' house,' Grace said. 'I guess with the wedding and then the emergencies coming in from the bus accident, no one's had time to secure that furniture.'

Harry was already turning the car that way.

'We'll do it before we start on our evacuations,' he said. 'Imagine some poor person seeking help at the hospital and being knocked out by flying furniture before he even gets there.'

He drove up the circular drive in front of the old

house that had originally been built as the Crocodile Creek hospital, and which now housed an assortment of hospital staff, parked at the bottom of the front steps and told Grace to stay where she was.

She took as much notice of this order as she had of his earlier orders to do this or that, and followed him through the downstairs area of the big building and out to where the garden furniture was indeed still around the pool.

'Just throw it in the pool,' Harry told her. 'It's safest in there and it'll get a good clean at the same time.'

He picked up a plastic table as he spoke and heaved it into the pool, following it with a sun lounge, while Grace took the smaller chairs and tossed them in.

'This is fun!' she said, grabbing the last chair and tossing it high so it made a satisfying splash.

'You find the weirdest things fun!' Harry grumbled at her, then he took her hand. 'Come on, let's have more fun—getting Mr and Mrs Aldrich to move out of their house.'

OK, so it was a protective gesture and meant nothing, especially in the context of getting over Harry, but holding hands with Harry felt so good Grace couldn't help but smile.

They ran back through the big recreation room under the doctors' house, out to the car. In the cove below the headland, the sea roared and tumbled, sending spray higher than the cliffs.

Willie was flexing his muscles.

CHAPTER SIX

'WHAT time's high tide?' Grace asked as they strapped themselves back into the vehicle.

'It was midnight, so it's going out now,' Harry said. 'I suppose we can be thankful for small mercies. The storm surge from the cyclone will be bad enough at low tide, but if it had coincided with a high tide, who knows how many places might have been washed away?'

They were driving past the pub as Harry spoke and Grace shivered, imagining a wave of water sweeping over the row of businesses beside it. The police station was directly behind the shops, although on a slight rise.

'Are you free to be doing evacuations?' Grace asked, thinking of the enormous task of co-ordination that must be going on, with the station at its hub.

'There's no room for me over there,' Harry replied, nodding towards the station. 'One of the benefits of getting a new building last year is that it's built to the stringent category five building regulations so all the staff who live in less well-constructed flats or houses have shifted their families in. It was part of our contingency plans and it works because it means I now have five trained staff there ready for emergencies and on standby for clean-up later, and also have enough people to cut down shifts on the radio to two-hourly.'

'Two-hourly shifts? Is that all they can take? Is it so tense?' Grace asked, wondering why she'd never thought about this aspect of an emergency. With the SES, all the members on duty had radios tuned to the police emergency frequency and although she and other team leaders radioed their members, they relied mainly on the police radio operator to co-ordinate their efforts.

'It's the radio operator who's under the most stress at the moment,' Harry explained. 'Taking emergency calls and relaying them to wherever they need to go, so being able to run two-hour shifts cuts down on tension and the possibility of mistakes. But having staff in the station also means I've got someone there whose sole task is to plot the cyclone's course, taking all the direction, speed and intensity readings from the Met and marking them on the map. He'll give me a call when Willie's an hour from crossing the coast and also get the radio operator to order any emergency crews off the streets. Once Willie's that close, anyone outside is in danger.'

Grace nodded her understanding. All her people had orders to return to their homes as soon as they'd evacuated the people on their lists. In times like this their families had to be their prime concern.

They were driving past the Grubbs' house and Grace nodded towards it.

'Good thing the hospital preparations included orders for all staff in older housing to take shelter there. The Grubbs' house always looks as if it will blow down in a strong wind or slide the rest of the way down the slope into the creek. Heaven knows what Willie will do to it.'

Harry looked towards the house where the hospital yardman lived with his wife, who was in charge of the housekeeping side of the hospital. The old place had been added onto so often it was starting to resemble a shed on an intensive chicken farm. The oldest part, nearest the creek, stood on timber stumps so old they'd shrunk so the veranda on that side and the small room they'd enclosed on it were cantilevered out from the rest of the house—the stumps taking none of the weight.

'Charles has been trying to talk them into letting him build them a new house for years, but the Grubbs refuse, saying the place suits them as it is.'

'Or until it blows down,' Grace commented, then, as Harry slowed down at an even older house further along the street, she wondered how it would feel to be so attached to a dwelling you wouldn't want to change it—or leave it in a cyclone.

Was that what 'home' was all about?

Although her stepmother had always been kind, the concept of home had eluded Grace. Sometimes in her dreams she saw it as a whitewashed cottage set amid green fields, but that was wrong. She knew she'd lived in Belfast and had seen enough pictures of the city to know there was nary a field nor a cottage in sight.

'You're too tired to be doing this!'

Harry's cross exclamation brought her back to the present. He was frowning anxiously at her, and his hand was warming the skin on her forearm.

'Not tired, just thinking,' she told him, pressing her hand over his. 'Thinking about homes.'

Harry shook his head and got out of the car. Why would such a simple remark—thinking about homes—get under his skin?

Because he now knew Grace had never really had a home?

But should that make him want to wrap his arms around her and hold her tight against his body?

He couldn't blame physical attraction for this urge, because it wasn't part of the equation. Not this time…

He'd parked so the passenger door was away from the wind, making it easier for Grace to get out, although walking to the front door of the old weatherboard house was a struggle, so he kept an arm protectively around her shoulders.

Mrs Aldrich greeted them with a battery-powered lantern held at shoulder height, the light good enough to show a tear-stained face *and* the attitude of belligerence written across it.

'I've got this lantern and torches and water and biscuits in the bathroom and Karen from next door has taped my windows and I'm not going,' she said, and Harry heard Grace sigh as if she understood the older woman's feelings and didn't want to argue.

'You have to, Mrs Aldrich.' Harry used his firm policeman voice. 'Your house just isn't safe. We need to move you and Bill down to the civic centre.'

'Bill's dead.'

Harry's stomach clenched. Another look at Mrs Aldrich's face told him this was true.

Floored by this unexpected development, Harry

could only stare at her. Fortunately Grace had more presence of mind.

'What happened?' she asked gently, stepping past Harry and putting her arm around the elderly woman, carefully guiding her further into the house.

'He just died,' Mrs Aldrich replied, her resolute voice abandoning her so the words quavered out. 'We knew it was close. I was sitting by him and he touched my hand like he was saying goodbye then that rattly breathing he'd had earlier just stopped.'

'Oh, Mrs Aldrich, I'm so sorry,' Grace said, completely ignoring the little hurry-up motions Harry was making with his hands. 'Have you had a cup of tea? Can I get you something? I should have a look at Bill, just to be sure. Do you mind?'

She hesitated, perhaps aware she was asking too many questions, then, as Harry wondered just how she'd handle this, she added another one.

'What if Harry makes you a cup of tea while you show me where Bill is?'

Harry wondered if she'd gone mad. OK, so Mrs Aldrich was in her nineties and she and Bill had been married for more than seventy years. Was Grace thinking they had to do this carefully if they didn't want another death on her hands?

'Strong, sweet tea,' she said to Harry, as she guided the older woman towards the rear of the house where the bedrooms were.

'Cyclone warnings are now hourly, Willie's due to hit us in two to three hours and instead of evacuating people I'm making tea,' Harry muttered to himself, but he'd known Bill and Daisy Aldrich all his life and his heart ached for Daisy and the sadness she must be feeling right now.

He made the tea, still muttering to himself, knowing in his gut that this wasn't the end of the Aldrich saga for the night.

'We've got to get her to the civic centre,' he whispered to Grace, who was sitting next to Daisy, beside the bed where Bill indeed lay dead.

'I heard that, Harry Blake,' Daisy countered. 'Seventy years Bill and I have shared this house, our kids were born here, the roof's blown off in other cyclones, but it's survived. So if you think I'm leaving Bill alone here tonight then you're very much mistaken.'

For one wild moment Harry considered the possibility of taking a dead body to the safe haven of the civic centre, then he saw Grace shake her head and wondered if she'd read his thoughts.

Of course they couldn't. All their attention had to be on the living, but he knew he'd have a battle on his hands moving Daisy.

Grace was holding the cup to Daisy's lips, encouraging her to drink, while Harry stood helplessly beside her, anxious to keep moving, knowing there was so much still to do.

'Harry, would you get a thick bedcover from one of the other beds? I'll wrap it around Mrs Aldrich's shoulders so she's got some protection should a window go. And one for Bill as well.'

Glad to have something to do, Harry went through to another bedroom where both the single beds had thick coverlets.

He brought them back and watched as Grace placed one carefully over Bill, folding down the top of it so they could still see his face.

'If the window breaks or the roof goes, you can pull it up,' she said to Daisy, now wrapping the second bedcover around the frail old woman. 'Harry and I will try to get back—or one of us will—to sit with you. But if we don't, use the cover to protect yourself, and if things get really wild, get under the bed.'

Daisy smiled through the tears that seeped down her face.

'Bill always said he'd protect me, no matter what,' she said, then she touched Grace's cheek. 'You're a good girl. If that Harry had a scrap of sense he'd have snapped you up a long time ago.'

Grace bent and touched her lips to the lined cheek.

'You take care,' she said, then she led a bemused Harry out of the room.

'You're going to leave her there? Not even argue about it? We can't just give in like that?'

'Can't we?' Grace said softly. 'Think about it, Harry. How important is her life to her right now? I know in a month or so, when the worst pain of her grief has passed, she'll find things she wants to live for, but at the moment she has no fear of death—in fact, she'd probably welcome it. And look at it from her point of view—Bill's been her whole life, how could she possibly go off and leave him now?'

Harry began to reply but Grace had turned back towards the bedroom, fishing her mobile phone out of her pocket as she went.

'Here,' she said, offering it to Mrs Aldrich. 'The

phone lines are all down but the cellphones will still work. This one is programmed to reach Harry's cell-phone, the one he's carrying today. Just press the number 8 and it will ring through to Harry.'

'Won't you need the phone?' Harry demanded, although what he wanted to know was who had the number one to seven positions on Grace's cellphone.

He knew she didn't have a mother…

'I've got my radio,' she reminded him, 'and just about everyone at the civic centre will be clutching their mobiles so they can report on conditions to their relatives in far-flung places or sell their phone pictures to television stations. I think I'll manage without one.'

'Because you've no relatives in far-flung places?' Harry asked, disturbed that the question of family and Grace had never occurred to him before tonight's revela-tions.

'Because I'll be far too busy to be phoning anyone,' Grace replied. 'Come on, we've people to evacuate.'

They ran from the house to the car, and he struggled to open the door and let her in, but even if conversation had been possible he wouldn't have known what to say. In some vague way he sensed that Grace was right about leaving Daisy where she was, but for so long his practical self had ruled his emotional self that it took a little bit of adjusting to accept emotion might have a place even in emergency situations.

Fortunately the next four couples were more easily moved, and by the time they had the last of them settled in the civic centre, everyone had been checked off the evacuation list.

Harry looked around the crowded area. Babies cried,

and small children, excited by the different location and the thrill of being awake in the early hours of the morning, ran around excitedly. Somewhere a dog barked, and a cockatoo let out a loud squawk of complaint, but most of the refugee pets were as well behaved as their human owners.

'At least the majority took note of what we said, about making sure they had animal carriers for their pets as part of their cyclone preparations.'

Grace was by his side and he nodded, acknowledging it had been a good idea. The circular dropped in the letterbox of every dwelling in town had not only been an initiative of the SES, but had been delivered by the volunteers.

'Where's Sport?' she asked, looking at a small kelpie cross who was protesting loudly about his accommodation.

'He's at my parents' place. I couldn't risk leaving him in the house when I knew I wouldn't be there.'

'Bet he's furious he's missing all the fuss,' Grace said, and Harry smiled. He'd rescued the small kelpie pup from the local rubbish dump after a wild thunderstorm. Whether he'd been abandoned because of an injury to one leg, or the injury had happened during the storm, Harry didn't know. He'd paid to have the leg treated, and when that hadn't worked, the leg had been amputated. He'd intended giving the dog away, but the fiercely loyal animal had had other ideas, finding his way back to Harry's no matter where he'd been taken.

In the end, his sheer determination had persuaded Harry to keep him.

'I need to check on a few people,' Grace said, and

moved into the small corridor between sleeping bags, mattresses and assorted padding brought along by the evacuees.

He watched her bend to speak to a heavily pregnant woman who should probably have been at the hospital rather than here, then, mindful that watching Grace was not his job right now, he walked through to the kitchen area where volunteers were making sandwiches and handing out tea or coffee to anyone who wanted it. He grabbed a cup of coffee and a sandwich, thinking Grace was probably in need of sustenance as well.

She was at the far end of the hall, talking to one of her SES crew, her arms waving in the air as she explained some detail. And although she was wearing plain cargo trousers and a T-shirt, all Harry could see was a curvy figure in two scraps of blue lace.

Muttering to himself once again, he took his coffee into one of the meeting rooms so he could concentrate on the messages coming through on his radio. Reports told him where power lines were down and where the emergency crews on duty were handling problems. The hour when the radio operator would order everyone into safe shelters, whether at their homes, at the police station or here at the civic centre, was fast approaching. Another report told him the hospital had been switched over to generator power, and even as that message came through the lights went out in the civic centre.

There was a momentary darkness, which caused the kids to scream with pretend fear, then the generators kicked in and the lights flickered back to life, but that instant of darkness had reminded Harry of the blackout earlier.

Had reminded him of kissing Grace…

'Boy, this food is good! It's the roast lamb from the wedding. Apparently, after we left, Mrs P. set the remaining guests to making sandwiches with the leftover food. Some was delivered to the hospital and the rest here.'

Grace was munching on a sandwich as she came up behind Harry. Everything had been OK between them—maybe a trifle strained but still OK—while they'd been caught up in rescuing Troy and getting off the mountain. Then, apart from a slight altercation over sleep, while they'd organised the evacuations. But now, in this lull before the storm—literally—she wasn't sure just where she stood with Harry.

Knew where she should stand—far, far away.

'We've got about ten of the less injured people from the bus here,' she said, taking another bite of sandwich and chewing it before getting back to the conversation. 'Apparently all the belongings we gathered up at the accident site were taken to Reception at the hospital. By now most of the stuff belonging to the hospitalised people will have been matched up to them, so I wondered if we could go over and collect the rest—it must belong to those who are here and I'm sure they'll all feel better if they have their own belongings with them.'

Harry shook his head, unable to believe he'd forgotten about the stuff he'd packed into the back of his vehicle.

'It's not at the hospital, it's here. I'll grab an able-bodied male and go get it from the car.'

'Get two able-bodied men and let them do it. Take a break,' Grace suggested, but Harry wasn't listening, already talking to one of the locals who then followed him out of the hall.

Grace followed him to the door, waiting until the two men brought in the luggage and handbags, then she spread it out so people could identify their belongings. The bus passengers, recognising what was going on, moved through the crowded room, then one by one they swooped on personal possessions, every one of them clutching the piece of luggage to their chests, as if they'd found lost treasure.

'It's a security thing,' Grace murmured, thinking how she'd clutched Harry's dinner jacket—remembering she'd left it in a sodden heap on her living-room floor.

Slowly the pile diminished until all that remained was a new-looking backpack.

'I wonder if the shoe belongs to that one,' Harry said, and knelt beside it, opening the fastening at the top and spilling out the contents.

'Damn it to hell!' Grace heard him whisper, as he pushed small shorts and T-shirts into one pile and some women's clothing into another. 'There *is* another child!'

'That's my dog!'

Max knew he should be pleased he'd finally found Scruffy, but the kid from the bus was clutching the dog against his chest and looked as if he'd never let him go.

All eyes, the kid. Huge eyes Max could see even though it was as dark as dark could be.

The kid was crouched under a tree fern—stupid place to shelter 'cos the water came straight through the leaves of tree ferns.

'Come on,' he told the kid. 'We've got to find the road. Or get back to the bus so we can get out of the rain.'

The kid shook his head and must have squeezed Scruffy tighter because Scruffy gave a yelp.

'You can hold the dog,' Max offered, and watched while the kid considered this. Then he stood up and Max saw his feet. One foot—bare—the other in a sneaker, the bare one cut and scratched and probably bleeding, although it was too dark to see the red of blood.

Everything was black.

'Hang on,' he told the kid and he sat down and took off his sneakers, then his socks, then he pulled his sneakers back on over his bare feet. Hard 'cos they were wet.

'You have the socks,' he told the kid. 'Put both on your foot that's lost its shoe. I'd give you my shoe but it'd be too big. Go on, sit down and do it. I'll hold the dog.'

The kid sat and reluctantly gave up his hold on Scruffy, though when Max hugged his pup against his chest Scruffy gave a different yelp.

'He's hurt,' Max whispered, holding the dog more carefully now.

The kid nodded, but he was doing as he was told, pulling on one sock then the other over it.

The dog was shivering so Max tucked him inside his T-shirt, then he reached out and took the kid's hand.

He'd walked downhill from the bus, so it and the road must be uphill.

'Let's go, kid,' he said, hoping he sounded brave and sensible. Sensible was good, he knew, because Mum always kissed him when she said he'd been sensible.

And brave was good. All the knights he read about were brave.

He didn't feel brave. What he felt was wet and cold and scared…

CHAPTER SEVEN

GRACE watched as Harry reached for his cellphone and dialled a number, then shook his head in disgust and slammed the offending machine back into his pocket.

Whoever he was phoning must be out of range.

Now he pulled his radio out and began speaking into it, calling to someone, waiting for a reply, calling someone to come in.

Urgently!

Harry put the radio away and began repacking the clothing into the backpack, folding small T-shirts with extraordinary care. Grace watched him work, but as he pulled the cord tight and did up the catch on the top, she could no longer ignore the anguish on his face.

She knelt beside him and took the capable hands, which had trembled as he'd folded clothes, into hers.

'Are there kids out there? Do you know that for sure?'

He nodded.

'Georgie's Max we know for sure, and now this.'

He pulled the little sneaker from his pocket, poking the tip of his finger in and out of the hole that made up the eye of the fish painted on it.

'Two kids.'

Despair broke both the words.

'We can go back,' Grace suggested, urgency heating her voice. 'Go and look for them.'

'I *can't* go, and logically nor can you. You're a team captain—this cyclone will pass and we'll both be flat out sorting the damage and running rescue missions.'

He took a deep breath, then eased his captured hand away from hers.

'Georgie's gone to look—she and Alistair. We'll just have to hope they're in time.'

In time—what a dreadful phrase.

But the second child?

'If there's a second child unaccounted for, why has no one mentioned it? Why has no one said my child's missing?'

One possible answer struck her with the force of a blow.

'The woman who died? Oh, Harry, what if it's her child?'

'That's what I've been thinking,' Harry said bleakly, 'although there's a woman at the hospital who's in an induced coma at the moment, so maybe the child belongs to her. And the woman who died had a boy-friend—surely he'd have mentioned a child.'

Grace tried to replay the rescue scene in her mind—a badly injured woman *had* been rescued early in the proceedings. Susie's sister, who'd acted as a bridesmaid at the wedding, had been looking after her.

'Let's hope it's her and that she lives and that Georgie finds both kids,' Grace said, although this seemed to be asking an awful lot.

Worry niggled at her mind—two children lost in the bush in a cyclone?

Worry was pointless, especially now with Willie so close. There were things she had to do. She looked around at the people settling down to sleep, at the two paramedics and four SES volunteers, not sleeping, watchful.

'Everything's under control here. If you wouldn't mind giving me a lift, I'll go back to Mrs Aldrich's place and sit out the blow with her.'

'Sit out the blow?' Harry echoed. 'It's obvious you've never been in a cyclone. The whole house could go, Grace.'

'So I can give her a hand to get under the bed. I had a look at that bed. It's an old-fashioned one, with solid timber posts on the corners and solid beams joining them. Safe as houses—safer, in fact, than some of the houses in this town.'

'And you talk about me taking risks?' Harry muttered, but as he, too, had been worried about Daisy Aldrich—in between worrying about two children— maybe it wasn't such a bad idea. Only…

'You stay here, I'll go and sit with her,' he said and knew it was a mistake the moment the words were out of his mouth.

'We've already been through the hero thing a couple of times tonight! But not this time, Harry. Mrs Aldrich is my responsibility—'

The ringing was barely audible in the general hubbub of the room. Harry pulled his cellphone out of his pocket and checked the screen.

'Your number,' he said to Grace as he lifted the little phone to his ear and said a tentative hello.

'Harry, Daisy Aldrich. Karen from next door is here and she's having her baby and it's early and she can't get hold of Georgie who's not at the hospital or at home so can Grace come?'

'We'll be right there,' Harry promised, closing his phone and motioning to Grace.

'You win,' he said. 'We need a nurse. Daisy's next-door neighbour is having a baby.'

'Karen? I saw her last week when she came for a check-up. She's not due for three or four weeks.'

'Tell the baby that,' Harry said, leading the way out of the hall.

Daisy was in her kitchen, boiling water on a small gas burner when Grace and Harry arrived.

'I don't know why people boil water,' she said, waving her hand towards the simmering liquid. 'No one ever did anything with boiling water when I was having my babies.'

A cry from the back of the house reminded them of why they were there.

'We dragged a mattress into the bathroom and she's lying on that. She'd never have got under the bed, the size she is.'

Grace was already hurrying in the direction of the cry. Another battery lantern was barely bright enough to light the room, but Grace could see the shadowy shape that was Karen, hunched up on the mattress which had been placed between the wall and an old-fashioned, claw-footed bath.

Fluid made dark smears across the mattress, but before Grace could check if it was water from the birth sac or blood, Karen cried out again, helplessly clutching the edge of the bath, her body contorting with pain.

'It hurts too much,' she said. 'Make it stop. Please, make it stop.'

Grace knelt beside her, sliding her hand around to rest on Karen's stomach, feeling the rigidity there.

'How long have you been having contractions?' she asked Karen as the stomach muscles relaxed.

'This morning,' the girl sobbed, 'but I thought they were those pretend ones with the silly name. The baby's not due for three weeks. And everyone was telling me first babies are always late so they had to be the pretend contractions.'

'Have you timed them at all?' Grace asked, trying to unlock Karen's death grip on the bath so she could lay the young woman down to examine her.

'No!' Karen roared, crunching over in pain again. 'You time them!'

She puffed and panted, occasionally throwing out combinations of swear words Grace had never heard before.

Grace pulled a towel off the towel rail, then looked around to see Harry and Mrs Aldrich peering in through the door.

'Could you find something soft to wrap the baby in? And some spare towels would be good. And scissors, if you have them,' she said, then looked at Harry.

'How long do we have before Willie arrives?'

'Three quarters of an hour, according to the latest alert. He's also been upgraded—definitely a category five now.'

He looked around at the walls and ceiling of the bathroom.

'This room's too big for safety—the load-bearing walls are too far apart—although the bath looks solid enough.'

But Grace's attention was back on Karen, who with a final shriek of pain had delivered a tiny baby boy.

He was blue, but as Grace cleared mucous from his mouth and nose, he gave a cry and soon the bluish skin turned a beautiful rosy pink.

'You little beauty,' Grace whispered to him, holding him gently in the towel.

Mrs Aldrich returned with the scissors, more towels and a soft, well-worn but spotlessly clean teatowel.

'That's the softest I've got,' she said, peering into the room then giving a cry of surprise when she saw the baby. 'It's the way of the world—one dies and another takes his place,' she said quietly, then she padded away, no doubt to sit beside her Bill.

'I'll call him William Harry,' Karen said, as Grace wrapped the baby in the teatowel and handed him to Karen, suggesting she hold him to her breast. But Karen didn't hear, her eyes feasting on the little mortal in her arms, her attention so focussed on his tiny form Grace had to blink away a tear. 'William after Bill, who was always kind to me, and Harry after Harry because he was here.'

Grace looked up at Harry who was pale and tense, shaking his head as if he didn't want a baby named after him. But even as Grace wondered about this reaction she became aware of the roaring noise outside the house and understood his lack of emotion. Another William— Willie—was nearly on them.

She turned her attention back to Karen, massaging

her stomach to help her through the final stage of labour, then cutting and knotting the cord and cleaning both mother and child.

Harry returned as she tucked a towel around the pair of them. He was carrying one of the bedcovers he'd found earlier, a pillow and a couple of blankets.

'I'm going to put these in the bath, Karen, then I want you and the baby to get in there. We'll put the mattress over the top to keep you both safe from falling debris. You'll still be able to breathe and it's not heavy, so if you feel claustrophobic you can lift it up a bit.'

Karen and Grace both stared at him, Karen finding her voice first.

'In the bath?'

Harry, who was making a nest of the blankets and bedcover, nodded.

'It's an old cast-iron bath—far too heavy to move even in a cyclone. Its high sides will protect you both and support the mattress. I wouldn't do it but the house has already lost a bit of roof and the walls are moving.'

Karen stopped arguing, handing the baby to Harry to hold while she stood up and clambered into the bath. Grace helped her, leaning over to make sure she was comfortable. She turned to Harry to take the baby and the look of pain and despair on his face made her breath catch in her lungs.

'I'll give him to Karen,' Grace said gently, moving closer so she could take the little bundle. Harry's eyes lifted from the baby to settle on Grace's face, but she knew he wasn't seeing her—wasn't seeing anything in the present.

Had there been a baby? she wondered as he stepped

forward and leant over, very gently settling the baby in his mother's arms.

Then he straightened up and strode out of the room, returning seconds later with a light blanket, which he tucked around the pair of them.

Karen smiled at him then tucked the baby against her breast, murmuring reassuringly to the little boy, although Grace knew the young woman must be terrified herself.

'Here,' Grace said, fishing in her pocket for the bottle of water and a couple of health bars. 'Something to eat and drink while Willie blows over.'

Karen smiled and took the offerings, setting them down on her stomach, but her attention was all on the baby at her breast.

With Grace's help Harry lifted the mattress onto the top of the bath, leaving a little space where Karen's head was so she could see out.

'Put your hand up and move the mattress so I know you can,' he said, and Karen moved the mattress first further back then up again so only the tiny space was visible.

'You OK?' Grace asked, sliding her fingers into the space and touching Karen's fingers.

'I think so,' the young woman whispered, her voice choked with fear.

'We'll just be next door, under Daisy's bed,' Harry told her, then he put his arm around Grace's shoulders and drew her out of the room.

'I hate leaving her like that. Surely we should all be together,' Grace said, looking back over her shoulder at the mattress-covered bath.

'Better not to be,' Harry said, and Grace shivered as she worked out the implications of that statement.

Daisy met them as they entered her bedroom, and handed Grace the cellphone.

'Give it to Karen. And this torch. Tell her about pressing 8 to talk to Harry. It might make her feel less lonely.'

Grace turned, but Harry stopped her, taking both the cellphone and the torch.

'You help Daisy down onto the floor. If she lies on the mat I can pull her under the bed if we need the extra protection. And turn off your radio. I'm turning mine off as well. There's nothing anyone can do out there, so we might as well save batteries.'

He walked away, leaving Grace to put a pillow on the mat, then help the frail old woman down onto the floor.

'Cover Bill so things don't fall on him,' she whispered to Grace, and Grace did as she asked, drawing the bedcover over the peaceful face of the man on the bed. Then she sat on the floor and held Mrs Aldrich's hand while outside the house the world went mad.

'We're going under the bed,' Harry announced, returning with the second mattress from the spare bedroom. 'I'm putting this on top as extra padding.'

He arranged the mattress so it rested from the bed to the floor, making a makeshift tent, then pulled the mat to slide Mrs Aldrich under the big bed.

'Your turn,' he said to Grace, who slid beneath the bed, leaving room for Harry between herself and the older woman.

Harry eased himself into the small space, wondering what on earth he was doing there when he could be in a nice safe police station or civic centre hall.

That it had to do with Grace he had no doubt, but he couldn't think about it right now. Right now he had to get these women—and the baby—through the cyclone.

He put his arm protectively around Daisy, but she shrugged him off.

'For shame, Harry Blake, and with Bill in the room. If you want to cuddle someone, cuddle Grace. She looks as if she could do with an arm around her, and you certainly need a bit of loving.'

Mrs Aldrich's voice was loud enough for Harry to hear above the roar of the approaching force, but would Grace have heard?

And if she had and he didn't put his arm around her, would she think—?

He had no idea what she'd think. Somehow this wild, erratic force of nature had blown the two of them into totally new territory.

Territory where he *did* need a bit of loving?

Surely not.

But just in case Grace had heard—or maybe just in case he did need loving—he turned so he could put his arm around Grace, and when she didn't object he drew her closer, tucking her body against his and once again feeling her curls feathering the skin beneath his chin.

'Cuddling me, Harry?' she said, her light, teasing voice defeating the noise outside because her lips were so close to his ear. 'Aren't you afraid? I mean, if a shuffling dance provoked the deadly physical attraction, what might a cyclone cuddle do?'

She was making fun of him, but still it hurt, and

somehow, because this was Grace and maybe because Bill and Daisy had loved one another for seventy years or maybe even because within minutes they could all be dead, he started telling her.

'We'd known each other for ever, Nikki and I, our parents friends enough for me to call hers Aunt and Uncle. She left town to go to university in Townsville while I went to Brisbane for my training. Then, about three and a half years ago, her parents were killed in a car accident. She came home to see to everything, I helped her—well, my parents arranged everything for her, but I was there for comfort.'

Grace felt his arms tighten around her, and kept as still as she could. She wasn't sure if she really wanted to hear about him loving Nikki, but listening to Harry was definitely better than listening to the raging fury of the cyclone and wondering if any of them would survive.

And maybe he needed the catharsis…

'Comfort is physical, as you know, and suddenly we both felt the attraction that being close had stirred. Wild attraction, heightened most probably on Nikki's side by grief.'

He paused then added in an undertone, 'I didn't have that excuse.

'We thought it love, Grace, and married, caught in a whirl of physical delight that left no room for plans or practicality, then, as suddenly as it had come, it seemed to leave. Not the physical attraction—that was always there—but when we weren't in bed there was— I can only describe it as an emptiness. Nikki was still grieving for her parents and she also missed her job, while I spent more time than was necessary at mine.'

Grace turned in his arms so she could hold him. She told herself it was because the noise of the cyclone was as loud as an express train roaring through a tunnel, but really it was so she could rub her hands across his back, offering silent sympathy he might or might not want.

Her heart ached for him—for the pain she heard in his voice and in the silence that now lay between them. But she couldn't prompt him, knowing he had to get through this story his own way.

'We didn't talk about it—in fact, I didn't know if Nikki felt it—but I was gutted, Grace, to think I'd mucked up so badly. Then I thought about it—really thought about it—and decided it would all be OK—that we could work it out. We'd always loved each other as friends, so surely that would remain as a solid foundation, and we had compatibility, so that had to count in building a future…'

He paused again and she felt his chest fill with air then empty on a sigh. She tightened her arms around him, offering the only comfort available.

'Eventually she told me she'd been offered a new television job in Brisbane. She'd been with the same station in Townsville but this was a promotion. Would I transfer to the city to be with her?'

Somewhere outside a tortured screeching noise suggested a roof was being torn apart. Mrs Aldrich's roof?

Grace snuggled closer, fear moving her this time.

'Go on,' she prompted, knowing Harry's story was probably the only thing holding at bay the terror that was coiled within her.

'I said I would, wanting so much to make it work, although all my life all I'd ever wanted was to be a policeman here where I belonged. We made arrangements, looked at housing on the internet, then she went to Townsville to see her old boss.'

The story stopped, and with it the noise.

'It's over?' Grace whispered, then heard how loud her voice sounded in the silence and realised she hadn't whispered at all.

'It's the eye passing over,' Harry told her as he slid out from under the bed and cautiously lifted the mattress aside. 'You two stay right where you are. I'll check on Karen and the baby and be straight back.'

Grace reached out to stop him, but it was too late, so she had to wait, fearful for his safety, having heard enough of cyclones to know that the eye was only the calm before the storm returned, only this time the wind would blow the other way.

'Both sound asleep, would you believe,' Harry reported as the howling, roaring noise drew close again. 'I guess having a baby and being born are both tiring experiences.'

He slid beneath the bed, lying between the two women, reporting to Mrs Aldrich that her kitchen roof had gone and a part of the bathroom wall had been damaged, but generally things looked OK. Radio calls to the station had assured him everything was OK there and at the civic centre.

'It's the second blow, once everything is loosened, that knocks houses about,' Mrs Aldrich told him, as they all squiggled around to relieve cramped muscles and tired bones. 'Will you go on talking, Harry?' she added. 'I can't hear the words but I like to hear your voice—it's very soothing and it makes the cyclone noise easier to bear.'

Horrified that Daisy had even heard his voice, Harry hesitated, but the cyclone was roaring again, and Grace had snuggled close, so it was easy to finish the tale he'd carried inside him for so long, locked away but probably festering because it hadn't ever been told.

He tucked Grace closer, held her tightly, and blurted out the words.

'She went to Townsville to have an abortion.'

There, it was said.

For the first time he'd actually told someone about the almost routine operation that had led to the discovery of Nikki's inoperable cancer.

He felt Grace stiffen, then her hand crept up to touch his face, cupping his cheek in her palm.

'No wonder seeing that new baby hurt you,' she whispered, her voice choked with tears.

He shook his head although he knew neither woman would see the gesture, frustrated at this situation. What was he thinking, lying under a bed—a bed with a dead body in it—in a category five cyclone, playing out his past like a series of episodes in a soap opera?

Fortunately—for his sanity—at that moment the roar grew louder and above the wild fury of the wind they heard the scream of metal sheets being torn from their anchors, nails screeching in protest as the rest of Daisy's roof peeled away.

'The weight of rain could bring the ceiling down so we stay here until we know the wind has eased,' Harry warned the two women, reaching out and drawing both of them closer, knowing they all needed human contact at the moment. 'Now Willie's crossed the coast, he'll lose his power.'

But what had that power done as it passed over the town? What havoc had it caused?

Anxiety tightened all the sinews in his body— anxiety for all the townsfolk but most of all for two small children out there on the mountain.

Had Georgie and Alistair reached them in time?

Were all four safe?

Max watched the light creep into the blackness of the hole in which they huddled, turning the dark shadows that had frightened him in the night into harmless posts and odds and ends of timber.

The kid was sleeping, curled up in a puddle of muddy-looking water, Scruffy in his arms. The kid had needed Scruffy, not because he'd said anything but because the way his face had looked when Max had heard Georgie calling to them and he'd answered her.

Instead of being happy they'd been found, the kid had started crying. Not bawling loudly, like CJ sometimes did when he was hurt, but silent crying, the light from the torch Mum was shining on them picking out the tears running down his face.

Max had thought at first he was crying because Mum had said she couldn't get them out straight away because it was too dangerous and that they'd have to wait until the cyclone stopped blowing trees over. But the kid had kept crying even after Mum had thrown down her leather jacket and some chocolate bars, and

Max had figured out he was crying because his Mum wasn't there.

So Max gave him Scruffy to hold because earlier, when Max had had a little cry because Mum wasn't there, holding Scruffy had made him feel really, really brave.

Max pushed the leather jacket over the sleeping kid and waited for more light to come.

CHAPTER EIGHT

It was another hour before the noise abated sufficiently for Harry to slide out from under the bed. The roof had indeed gone and the ceiling had collapsed in the far corner of the room, pouring water onto the floor, but thankfully the rest of the room was, for the moment, dry.

Grace joined him, staring about her at the devastation, then heading for the door.

'Don't go,' he said, catching her hand. 'You stay here with Daisy while I check out what's solid and what isn't.'

She turned, anxious eyes scanning his face in the murky dawn light.

'Be careful,' she said, touching her hand to his cheek, so many things unspoken in the gesture that Harry felt a hitch in his breathing.

The house was a mess. One of the bathroom walls had collapsed across the bath, so Harry had to toss boards and beams aside to get to the mattress-covered bath. Fortunately the ceiling had held so the room was relatively dry. He could hear Karen and the baby both crying, Karen hysterical when he lifted the mattress.

'Come on, I'll help you out. You can shelter in the bedroom with Daisy until it's safe enough to drive you to the hospital.'

'With Daisy and dead Bill? I can't do that. I can't take my baby into the room with a dead person.'

Harry sighed but he kind of understood. There'd been ghosts beneath that bed with him.

'All right, but I'll have to put the mattress back on top of you.'

'That's OK,' Karen said, stifling her sobs and settling back down in her nest of blankets. 'Now it's getting lighter and I know you're not all dead and that noise has stopped, it's not nearly as scary.'

He replaced the mattress—if the ceiling did come down he didn't want wet plasterboard smothering the pair of them—then did a recce through the rest of the house. To his surprise, the dining room, a square room to one side of the kitchen, was apparently unscathed, and from the kitchen he could see that the roof in that area remained intact.

Once they had tarpaulins over the rest of it, Daisy might be able to move back into her home as soon as services like electricity, sewerage and water were restored, although that could be weeks away.

Sure his charges were safe, he ducked into the dining room, sat down on a chair and pulled out his cellphone. Time to check on the damage in the rest of the town.

Unbelievable damage from all accounts, the policeman on duty at the station told him, but no reports of casualties. Harry breathed a sigh of relief.

'Just let me sort out a few problems here,' he said, 'and then I'll do a run through town to see what's what.

Expect me back at base in about an hour. In the meantime I'll be on air on the radio or you can get me on the cellphone.'

He rang the hospital. No word from Georgie but they'd despatch an ambulance to pick up Karen, the baby and Daisy Aldrich. They'd also contact the funeral home to send a car for Bill.

Grace was standing in the doorway as he ended the call.

'*Did* she have the abortion because of her career?' she asked, and the question was so unexpected he answered without thinking.

Answered honestly.

'No,' he said bleakly, remembering the terrible day he'd stared in disbelief at Nikki while she'd told him this—and then, disbelief turning to denial, added that she was dying of cancer. 'At least, she said not, but it might have had something to do with it. She said she had it because we didn't love each other. She said she knew that almost as soon as we were married—knew it was just lust between us, lust and her grief, and that I was there. She said she didn't want to bring a baby into that situation because without love we'd probably split up.'

Grace came closer and put her arms around him, holding him tightly.

'Then she told me about the cancer—that when she had the operation they found inoperable cancer.'

'She was dying of cancer?'

Harry nodded.

'Which made my anger at her—my fury that she'd gone ahead and aborted my child without discussing it with me—totally absurd. The baby wouldn't have lived anyway, but that fact couldn't penetrate the anger. I said things then that should never have been said— hard, hot, angry things, and through all that followed— her time at home and then in hospital—that was the guilt I had to carry. To have reacted with anger towards Nikki who'd been my friend for ever, to have hurt her at any time, let alone when she was dying…'

His shoulders hunched and he bent his head as if the weight of the emotional baggage he'd carried since that time still burdened his body.

'Physical attraction, Grace, do you wonder I'm suspicious of it?'

'But anger is a natural reaction to bad news,' Grace whispered to him. 'Your anger might have found an outlet in yelling about the abortion but it would have been far deeper than that—it would have been about the death sentence Nikki, your friend and lover, had just received.' She held him more tightly. 'It was natural, not cruel or unfair, Harry, and I'm sure Nikki would have understood that.'

'Would she?' he whispered hoarsely, the headshake accompanying the words telling Grace he didn't believe her.

The wailing cry of a siren told them the ambulance was close by. Grace let him go and headed for the door, wanting to help Karen and the baby out of the bath.

She heard the vehicle pull up, the sound of doors opening, the wheels on a stretcher dropping down.

'So now you know why he feels the way he does,' she muttered helplessly to herself, 'but what if it isn't just physical attraction?'

She understood so much more now—understood it was guilt and anger at himself that prompted not only Harry's risk-taking but also the emotional armour he'd drawn around himself.

Grace mulled it over as she led the paramedics first into the bathroom to collect Karen and baby William, then, once they were safely loaded, she walked with Daisy to the ambulance.

'Yes, I'll stay with Bill until the people from the funeral home arrive,' she promised Daisy, and was surprised at Daisy's protest.

'You'll do no such thing—you stay with Harry. Cyclone Willie shook a lot of things loose in that boy's heart. He's hurting and he needs someone with him.'

'As if Harry would ever admit to needing someone,' Grace said, but fortunately the funeral car arrived at that moment so she didn't have to make a choice.

Harry had returned to the dry refuge of the dining room while she'd been seeing the two vehicles depart. He looked grey with fatigue—or was it more than that? He looked...

Despairing?

'Georgie? You've heard from Georgie?'

He shook his head, then muttered, 'I'm thinking no news is good news out there. I told Alistair we'd left the vehicle beyond the fallen tree—they could have sheltered in that.'

But this not good but not precisely bad news did nothing to ease the knots of worry in his features.

'What's wrong?' Grace asked, walking towards him and reaching out to take his hands. Watching his face carefully, ready to read a too-easy lie.

But he didn't lie, saying only, 'It's Sport,' in a tone of such flat despair Grace thought her heart would break.

'Dead?' she whispered, then remembered where the dog had been. 'Your parents? They're OK?'

'Sport's not dead but gone. My parents are fine. Very little damage to the house, although the sheds have been destroyed and the sugar crop's flattened. But Sport's disappeared. Mum said he grew more and more agitated as Willie passed over, then, when Dad opened the door to look at the damage during the calm of the eye, Sport took off, last seen heading back towards the town.'

Grace pictured Harry's parents' place, not far from the sugar mill on the outskirts of town.

She could imagine the dog, hip-hopping his way through the fury of the cyclone.

Sport, a ragged, crippled mutt that had somehow wormed his way through the emotional barriers Harry had built around himself.

Wormed his way into Harry's heart.

She wrapped her arms around him and held him tightly.

'I love you, Harry,' she said, although it was the last thing she'd meant to say.

Bloody dog!

She was resting her head against Harry's chest so couldn't see his reaction, although she felt his chest move with a sharp intake of air.

'I know you don't want to hear that,' she added, anxious to get it all smoothed over and things back to normal between them again. 'But we've been through so much—touched by death then welcoming new life, our physical world destroyed around us—I had to say it, and it's OK because I don't expect you to love me back. I've got over love before and I'll get over this, but it needed to be said.'

One of his arms tightened around her and he used his free hand to tilt her chin, so in the rain-dimmed morning light she saw his face.

Saw compassion, which she hated, but something else.

Surprise?

Natural enough, but was it surprise?

Before she could make another guess, Harry bent his head and kissed her, his lips crushing hers with hot, hard insistence. She melted into the embrace and returned the kiss, letting her lips tell him, over and over again, just how she felt.

One corner of her mind was aware of the futility of it all, but this was Harry and right now he needed whatever physical comfort she could give him.

And *she* needed something that at least felt like love…

Perhaps a minute passed, perhaps an hour, although, looking at her watch as she pushed out of Harry's arms, Grace knew it hadn't been an hour.

Two, three minutes maybe—a short time out from all the chaos that lay both behind and ahead of them.

And if her heart cringed with shame that she'd told Harry how she felt—a confession prompted by pity that he'd lost his dog, for heaven's sake—then she was good enough at pretence by now to carry on as if the words had not been spoken.

Which, she knew, was what Harry would do…

'We've got to go. Sport will be looking for you,' she said, and Harry nodded.

'Damn stupid dog!'

'We'll look at your place first,' Grace said.

Harry turned towards her, frowning now.

Grace loved him?

'We can't go out looking for a dog,' he growled. 'I need to see the damage, talk to people, get arrangements going.'

Talk about coming out of left field! Grace, his friend, suddenly declaring love for him?

'You need to drive through town to see the damage,' this friend he suddenly didn't know reminded him, then she repeated what she'd said earlier. 'We'll go past your place first.'

And now carrying on as if she hadn't just dropped a bombshell on him.

As if love had never been mentioned.

He had to put it right out of his mind. The town and its people needed him—and needed him to have a fully functioning brain, not some twitchy mess of grey matter puzzling over love and Grace.

Grace first—he'd deal with Grace the friend and that way might not keep thinking about the Grace he'd kissed.

Twice…

'What's this *we?* I'll drop you home, that's if your cottage is still standing. Or at the hospital. You need to sleep.'

'No, Harry, we'll do a drive around town then you can drop me at SES Headquarters so I can start sorting out what's needed and who we've got to help.'

Unable to think of a single argument against this—well, not one that she would listen to—he led the way out to where he'd left the police vehicle, tucked in under the Aldrichs' high-set house. It seemed to have survived the onslaught with only minor damage.

Sadness filled her heart as Grace snapped her seat belt into place. She sent a sidelong glance at the object of her thoughts, who was talking seriously to someone on his cellphone. Now those fatal words had been said, they could never be unsaid, so things could never really be the same between them again.

That was probably just as well, because although she'd spoken lightly about getting over love, she knew this was going to take a huge effort, and not seeing much of Harry would certainly help.

Although, comparing what she'd felt for James with what she felt for Harry, maybe he was right about physical attraction giving an illusion of love.

Certainly the love she'd felt for James had never hurt like this…

It was at this stage of her cogitations that she became aware of the world around her—or what was left of it.

'I don't believe it,' she whispered, trying desperately to make some sense of the devastation that lay around them. Harry was driving very slowly and carefully, picking a path along a road strewn with corrugated iron, fibro sheeting, furniture and bedding, not to mention trees, branches and telegraph poles, the latter flung about as if they'd weighed no more than matches.

The rain poured down with unrelenting insistence, as if Nature hadn't yet done enough to bring the town of Crocodile Creek and its inhabitants to their knees.

'We'll need the army. The mayor phoned earlier. He's already asked the premier for help,' Harry said as he pulled into his driveway.

'But today?' Grace asked, staring helplessly around. 'What can we do today? Where do we start? How can we help people?'

'Food and water. I'll check Sport's not here, then drive around town. We'll stop at the civic centre first, although I've had a report that everyone's OK there. We're broadcasting messages asking anyone who needs help to get out of their house to phone the dedicated line at the police station—the number we gave out at the end of all the cyclone warnings.'

'Four, zero, six, six, eight, eight, nine, nine,' Grace repeated, remembering the trouble Harry had had getting a number so easy to remember.

The radio was chattering at them. All downed power poles and torn lines would have to be removed before the authorities would consider turning power back on. No reports of casualties so far, apart from those lost in the bus crash. Banana plantations and cane fields had been flattened. The farmers were in for a grim year, but Willie, his violence spent, had continued moving westward and was now dumping much-needed rain on the cattle country beyond the mountains.

'So Willie moves on,' Grace whispered as she heard this report. 'But how do people here move on? How can anyone move on from something like this?'

Harry glanced towards her, and she knew he was thinking of her stupid declaration.

Well, so what if he was? Like Willie, she was moving on.

Moving on…

CHAPTER NINE

THEY stopped at the house just long enough for Harry to satisfy himself Sport wasn't there. Neither was his dirt bike, which meant Georgie and Alistair were still out in the bush.

They were both sensible people, they had his vehicle out there to shelter in—or the bus—they'd be OK.

But had they found the kids?

· Worry knotted inside him and he sent a silent prayer heavenward, a plea that they and the two children were all right. Then he looked around at the havoc and wondered if heaven had given up answering prayers, because plenty of people had prayed the town would be spared a cyclone.

'Do you think the old bridge will hold?' Grace asked as they approached the bridge across the creek that separated the hospital part of the town from the main commercial and residential areas.

'The council engineers looked at it when it was forecast Willie might head this way and declared it would probably outlast the new bridge across the river, but the problem is, because it's low and water is already lapping at the underside, all the debris coming down the creek will dam up behind it, causing pressure that could eventually push it off its pylons.'

'Debris piling up is also causing flooding,' Grace said, pointing to where the creek had already broken its banks and was swirling beneath and around houses on the hospital side.

'Which will get worse,' Harry agreed, concern and gloom darkening his voice.

They were driving towards the civic centre now, Grace looking out for Sport, although the streets were still largely deserted.

Except for teenagers, paddling through floodwater on their surf-skis here and there, revelling in the aftermath of the disaster.

'I'll be in meetings for the rest of the morning,' Harry said, turning towards Grace and reaching out to run a finger down her cheek. 'You do what you have to do then get someone to run you home, OK? You need to sleep.'

'And you don't, Harry?' she teased, discomfited by the tenderness of his touch—by his concern.

'I can't just yet,' he reminded her, then he leant across the centre console and kissed her on the lips, murmuring, 'I'm sorry, Grace,' and breaking her heart one last time because the apology had nothing to do with not sleeping.

One of her fellow SES volunteers drove her home to check the cottage was all right. She'd lost a window and the living room was awash with water, her garden was wrecked, but apart from that she'd got off lightly. They drove on to SES Headquarters, passing people wandering through the wreckage of countless homes, oblivious of the rain still pelting down, looking dazed as they picked an object from the rubble, gazed at it for a moment then dropped it back.

Some were already stacking rubbish in a pile, hurling boards that had once made up the walls of their houses into a heap on the footpath. It would take forever to clear some of the lots, but these people were at least doing something. They were looking to bring some order back into their lives.

Once at Headquarters, she set up a first-aid station. Volunteers would be injured in the clean-up and would also know to bring anyone with minor injuries to the building.

What she hadn't expected was a snakebite.

'Bloody snake decided it wanted to share our bathroom with us. I had the kids in there,' the ashen-faced man told her. 'I picked it up to throw it out, and the damn thing bit me on the arm.'

He showed the wound, which Grace bandaged with pressure bandages, down towards the man's fingers then back up to his armpit.

But it was really too late for bandages. The wound had been oozing blood, and snake venom stopped blood clotting properly.

'Did you drive here?' she asked, and the man nodded, his breathing thickening as they stood there.

'Good. We'll take your car.'

She called two of the volunteers who'd come in looking for orders to carry the man out to the car.

'The less effort you make, the less chance of poison spreading.'

'It didn't look like a brown or taipan,' the man said, but Grace had already taken the car keys from his hand and was hurrying towards the door. Even so-called experts couldn't always identify snakes by their looks.

The volunteers settled her patient into the car, and she took off, making her way as fast as she could through the hazardous streets. At the hospital she drove straight into the emergency entrance, leaping out of the car and calling for a stretcher.

'Bringing your own patients, Grace?' someone called to her as she walked beside the stretcher.

'Snakebite,' she snapped, pushing the stretcher in the direction of a trauma room. 'We need a VDK.'

Inside the trauma room she started with the basics, knowing a doctor would get there when he or she could. She slipped an oxygen mask over her patient's head, opened his shirt and set the pads for electrocardiogram monitoring, and fitted an oxygen saturation monitor to one finger.

IV access next—they'd need blood for a full blood count and for a coag profile, urea, creatinine and electrolytes, creatine kinase and blood grouping and cross-matching. Urine, too—the venom detection kit worked on urine.

She talked to the man, Peter Wellings, as she worked, hoping a doctor would arrive before she got to the catheterisation stage.

A doctor did arrive, Cal Jamieson, looking as grey and tired as Grace was feeling.

She explained the situation as briefly as she could, then was surprised when Cal picked up a scalpel and turned to her.

'Where exactly was the bite?'

Grace pointed to the spot on the bandaged arm.

'And it was definitely bleeding freely?'

She nodded.

'OK, we can take a swab from there for venom detection, rather than wait for a urine sample. I'll cut a small window in the bandages, and in the meantime let's get some adrenaline for him in case there's a reaction to the antivenin—0.25 milligrams please, Grace. And get some antivenins ready—the polyvalent in case we can't identify the snake, and some brown, tiger and taipan, which are the most likely up here.'

Cal was working swiftly, cutting through the bandages, swabbing, talking to Peter as well as telling Grace what he required next. He took the swab and left the room, returning minutes later to go through the antivenins Grace had set out on a trolley.

'Tiger,' he said briefly, more to Grace than to Peter, who looked as if he no longer cared what kind of snake had bitten him. 'I'm going in strong because of the delay. The Commonwealth Serum Laboratories recommend one ampoule but we're going two. I've actually given three to someone who had multiple wounds. But he'll need careful monitoring—straight to the ICU once I've got the antivenin going in his drip.'

He glanced towards Grace as he worked.

'You've obviously been outside. How bad is it?'

Grace thought of the devastation she'd seen and shook her head.

'I can't describe it,' she said. 'I can't even take in what I've seen. All the photos of floods and hurricanes and even bomb-sites you've ever seen mixed into one. I don't know how people will begin to recover. And the rain hasn't let up one bit. That's making things worse.'

Cal nodded.

'We'll see plenty of post-traumatic stress,' he said. 'Hopefully we'll be able to get the staff we need to handle it—it's such a specialist area.'

He was adjusting the flow of the saline and antivenin mix, ten times the amount of saline to antivenin, and calibrating the flow so Peter would receive the mixture over thirty minutes.

Grace wrote up the notes, and the latest observations, wanting everything to be in order as Peter was transferred.

'He'll need to be on prednisolone for five days after it to prevent serum sickness,' Cal said, adding his notes. 'And watched for paralysis, which with tigers starts with muscles and tendons in the head.'

He was silent for a minute then added, 'And renal failure.'

Grace knew he was talking to himself, adding reminders as he would be the person caring for Peter in the ICU. Mistakes happened and were more likely when people were exhausted by extra shifts, and only by constant checking and rechecking would they be avoided.

'You staying?' he asked Grace.

'Am I needed?'

He shook his head.

'I think we've got things pretty well under control. The worst of the accident victims, a young woman called Janey, is coming out of her induced coma, and everyone else is stable so, no, if you're not on duty, buzz off home. You look as if you could do with about three days' sleep.'

'Couldn't we all?' Grace said, but she was grateful for Cal's dismissal. She could walk home and look for Sport on the way. Later she'd return to SES Headquarters for another shift, but she'd be a far more effective participant in the clean-up operation if she slept first.

She tapped on Jill's office door before she left, wanting to be one hundred per cent sure she wasn't needed.

'Go home and sleep,' Jill ordered in answer to Grace's query. 'You look as if you need about a week to catch up. Go!'

She waved her hands in a shooing motion.

'We've all been able to grab a few hours—mainly thanks to all the extra staff available because of the weddings. Joe's been marvellous, and even Christina has put in a couple of shifts on the monitors in ICU. They're both safe and sleeping at my place at the moment, in case you were worrying about them.'

Grace shook her head in amazement that she hadn't given her friends a thought for the last few hours, although she *had* known they were at the hospital and so had assumed they'd be safe.

'Some friend I am,' she muttered to herself as she left Jill's office, then her weary brain remembered Georgie and the children. She poked her head back around the door.

'Georgie?'

Jill frowned in reply.

'We think she's OK. A truckie out west picked up a message that would have been sent about the time the eye was passing over. Something about finding two children, but the signal kept breaking up so he didn't catch it all.'

Jill looked worried but Grace realised there was little they could do until they heard more.

The wind had eased off, but not the rain, so she took an umbrella from one of the stands at the entrance to Reception. She'd return it when she came back on duty, although so many umbrellas were left at the hospital no one would ever notice one was missing.

The scene outside hadn't improved. The Agnes Wetherby Memorial Garden between the hospital and the doctors' house had been flattened, but the old house stood, apparently having come through the violent cyclone unscathed. Grace didn't pause to check it thoroughly—her own home was calling to her.

But as she passed the big house on the headland, she looked down into the cove, staring stupidly at the waves crashing on the shore. It was low tide, there should be beach, but, no, the storm surge had pushed the water right up to the park that ran along the fore-shore so the beautifully ugly breadfruit trees and the delicate casuarinas that grew there now stood in water.

Every shop in the small shopping mall had lost its roof, while the Black Cockatoo looked as if it had lost most of its upper storey, although, from the sounds of revelry within, it was still open for business.

Grace turned down a side street, wanting to walk closer to the police station and Harry's house, hoping she'd see Sport.

Had the dog sensed Harry was in danger that it had taken off?

It seemed possible—

The scream was so loud and so fear-filled all thoughts of Harry and his dog fled. Grace turned in the direction it had come from and began to run, though to where she had no idea, until she turned a corner and saw the floodwaters. Filthy brown water swirling angrily along the street, washing under high-set homes and straight through those set lower.

Treetrunks, furniture, books and toys all rode the water, and further out something that looked like a garden shed sailed on the waters.

Another scream and this time Grace could pinpoint it. The Grubbs' house, Dora standing on her front veranda, water all around her, lapping at her feet, but seemingly safe, although she screamed and pointed and screamed again.

Grace pushed her way through shallow water towards the house, feeling how stupid it was to be carrying an umbrella with floodwaters up to her waist.

'No, no!' Dora cried, waving her arms when she saw Grace approaching. 'It's not me, it's the kids,' she yelled, pointing out into the maelstrom, towards the garden shed. 'The pantry broke off the house. I had the kids in there because it was safe and, look.'

'What kids?' Grace yelled, wondering if the cyclone had affected Dora's rationality. From what Grace had learned, Dora's 'kids' were in their thirties and living far from Crocodile Creek.

'CJ and Lily. I was minding them then Molly had the pups and the kids wanted to be there, and they're all in that room.'

Peering through the falling rain, Grace could almost imagine white, scared faces in the doorway of what she'd taken to be a shed.

'It will stop at the bridge,' she said to Dora. 'Have you got a cellphone?'

Dora shook her head.

'No matter, I've got a radio. Hopefully it's waterproof. I'll swim out to the kids and radio from there, but in the meantime, if anyone comes by, tell them to get onto the police and let them know to meet us at the bridge.'

Meet us at the bridge? she thought as she waded deeper and deeper into the murky water. As if they were going for a pleasure jaunt on the river.

Tourists went out on the river, but that was to look for and photograph crocodiles.

This was the creek, not the river, she reminded herself, but she still felt fear shiver up her spine.

'No,' she said firmly. 'Crocodiles have enough sense to stay out of flooded rivers *and* creeks.'

She bent into the filthy water to pull off her boots, then began to swim, setting her eyes on the floating bit of house, praying it would stay afloat at least until she got there.

The water fought her, pushing her one way and then another, making her task seem almost impossible. But then she looked up and saw the children. Cal's son, CJ, and Lily, Charles's ward, clinging to each other in the doorway of the floating room. Then CJ left the safety of the room, venturing out onto what must have been a bit more veranda, bending over as if to reach into the water.

'Stay back,' she yelled at him. 'Get back inside.'

He looked up as if surprised to see her, then pointed down to the water beside him.

'It's Sport!' he called, and Grace sighed as she splashed towards them. Now she had a dog to rescue as well.

'I'll get him,' she called to CJ, then she put her head down and ploughed through the last twenty metres separating her from the children.

Sport was struggling to get his one front foot onto the decking, and Grace grabbed him and boosted him up, then, fearful that her weight might unbalance the makeshift boat and bring them all into the water, she called to the kids to stay back as far as they could and eased her body up until she could sit on the wooden boards. Then, with caution, she got on to her hands and knees so she could crawl towards them.

She looked around, realising the pantry must once have been part of the veranda because a bit of veranda was still attached, working like an outrigger to keep the structure afloat.

For how long?

With legs and arms trembling either from the swim or fear, she hesitated, breathing deeply, trying to work out what might lie ahead.

She guessed they were maybe three hundred yards from the bridge, and she was reasonably sure the bridge would stop them, but whether it would also sink them was the question.

Kids first.

She crawled forward, wondering where Sport had gone, then entered the small room, where preserves and cereal and sauce bottles were jumbled in with two small children, two dogs, and too many newborn puppies for Grace to count.

'It's like being on a boat, isn't it, Grace?' CJ said as Grace knelt and wrapped her arms around the children.

'It is indeed,' she said, realising he'd been boosting Lily's confidence with talk of boats and adventure. CJ had never lacked imagination. 'And soon it's going to dock down at the bridge and we can all get off. I'm going to radio for someone to meet us there, OK?'

She detached the children, patted the wet Sport and the only slightly drier Molly—was Sport the father of this brood that he'd come through a cyclone to be with their mother? Did dog love work that way? Like human love?—and walked outside to radio SES Headquarters and explain the situation.

'Dora Grubb's been in touch,' Paul told her, 'and we've notified the police to be ready at the bridge. Have you any idea how you're going to get them off?'

'If all goes well and we don't sink, I'll pass the two kids over to rescuers then the pups and then the dogs.'

'Dogs?' Paul echoed weakly. 'Dora mentioned her dog Molly and some pups, but dogs?'

'Harry's Sport has joined the party,' Grace told him. 'Though what a policeman is doing with an un-neutered dog I'd like to know.'

'I guess Harry thought Sport had already lost a leg so didn't deserve to lose anything else,' Paul suggested.

Grace huffed, 'Men,' and stopped transmission.

Time to see to the kids and try to work out how to keep them all alive if their fragile craft sank.

Harry was in a meeting with local councillors, electricity officials and city engineers when he heard something different over the radio he had chattering quietly on the table beside him.

He'd been paying little attention to it, but had known he had to keep it on, half listening for any situation where he might be needed. Half listening for a report that Georgie and Alistair had returned with two kids.

But nothing so far.

Flood reports had begun to come in, but nothing serious as yet, until he heard a combination of words— flood, house, bridge, kids, and nurse from the hospital with them.

Instinct told him it was Grace and he turned the volume up a little, then, when he realised the transmission had finished, he excused himself to walk to a corner of the room and use his phone to call the station.

'No worries, Harry,' the constable who answered said. 'We've got it all under control. A bit of the Grubbs' house came adrift with a couple of kids inside, but Grace swam out to the kids and she's radioed in and reckons the room will stop when it hits the bridge. We'll have people there—'

'I'm on my way,' Harry said, anger and concern churning inside him. Grace accused him of taking risks and here she was, swimming through floodwaters filled with debris, snakes and crocodiles.

Stupid, stupid, stupid woman!

'Small crisis,' he said to the people gathered in the room as he strode out the door. Contingency plans could wait, or could be sorted without him—he needed to be on that bridge.

Which, please God, would hold.

How detailed had the engineer's inspection been? How minutely had he checked the structure?

He drove towards the bridge, passing more and more people on the rain-drenched streets, all with the bewildered expressions of disaster survivors. Rebuilding houses was one thing—could you rebuild people?

Maybe...

Maybe the anger he felt towards Grace was something to do with his own rebuilding process...

He swore at himself for such inane philosophising when his thoughts should be centred on rescue.

Swore at the Grubbs for their ridiculous habit of adding bits and pieces to their house—bits and pieces that could break off and be swept away by floodwaters. Damn it all, he'd seen that bit of the house—it had been ready to slide into the creek without the flood.

Then he was at the bridge and one look at the people gathered there made him shake his head. It was like a party—the fishing competition all over again. How word had got around he had no idea, but there must be fifteen people on the bridge with more arriving on foot and on surf-skis. And, far off, he could hear an outboard engine.

A boat! He should have thought of that first, but then he shook his head. With the debris in the water, whoever was running their outboard was also running the risk of hitting a submerged log and being tipped into the water.

Someone else to rescue.

He stopped the car and climbed out, looking upstream. One of his men came to stand beside him, explaining they'd stopped all traffic on the bridge and were getting the volunteers to spread out across it. Beyond his car an ambulance pulled up, then the hospital four-wheel-drive, a woman tumbling out.

The constable was saying something about ropes being in place and more equipment coming, but Harry barely heard, his eyes on the bobbing, slewing apparition riding the water towards them.

The craft looked for all the world like a Chinese junk floating on some exotic harbour, but then an eddy caught it and twirled it round and round, and above the raging noise of the water Harry heard a child's shrill scream.

His stomach was clenched so tightly it was like a boulder in his abdomen, and he wanted to plunge into the waters and swim towards the now teetering room.

'It's going to hit hard—let's get some tyres ready to give it some protection.'

Harry turned towards the man who'd spoken, recognising a member of Grace's SES team, then he saw Paul Gibson, looking grey and ill but there because a member of his service was in danger.

'There are tyres and rubber mooring buffers on the way,' Paul said, then pointed to an SES truck pulling up on the road at the end of the bridge. 'Or just arriving.'

More volunteers poured out of the truck, opening hatches to collect their booty. Soon they were walking across the bridge, mooring tyres and buffers in their arms.

'We'll wait until she gets closer,' Paul said, 'then work out where it's going to hit and use the protection there.'

Harry was glad to let him take charge. He was far too emotionally involved to be making cool decisions, and rescuing Grace and the children would need the coolest of heads.

Why he was so emotionally involved he'd think about later.

The wobbly room came closer, moving faster as the main current of the creek caught it and swirled it onward towards the bridge. He could see Grace now. She appeared to have wedged herself in the doorway of the room, and she had the two children clasped in her arms.

It made sense. All around town there were doorways still standing, the frames holding firm while the walls around them were blown to smithereens.

It looked like she was wearing a bikini, which, to Harry's dazed and frantic mind, seemed strange but still acceptable. Once he'd accepted a room floating on the creek, he could accept just about anything.

He moved across the bridge, trying to guess where they'd hit, needing to be right there to help her off.

And to rescue the children, of course.

A dog was barking.

Sport?

Harry peered towards the voyagers.

Grace couldn't have been stupid enough to swim out there for Sport?

Love me, love my dog?

His mind was going. It was the waiting. The room was barely moving now, pulled out of the main channel into an eddy. If he got a boat, they could row out to it.

The thought was turning practical when a child screamed again and the structure tipped, taking in water as it met the current once again, and this time hurtling towards the bridge.

Harry was there when it hit with such a sick crunching noise he couldn't believe it had stayed afloat. Now anger mixed with relief and his mind was rehearsing the lecture he was going to give Grace about taking risks.

He took a child, Lily, and passed her on to someone, took the other child, CJ, chattering away about his adventure but far paler than he should have been.

'I've got him,' someone said, and CJ was reefed out of his arms. He turned to see Gina, CJ's mother, clasping her son to her body, tears streaming down her face.

CJ kept talking but it was background noise. Harry's attention was on the rapidly sinking room.

'Here,' Grace said, coming out of the small room and passing a squirming sack to one of the SES men.

Not a bikini at all. It was a bra, but white, not blue.

Harry reached out to grab her but she disappeared inside again, returning with Sport, who saw Harry and leapt onto his chest. He fell beneath the weight of the dog's sudden assault, and was sitting on the bridge, comforting Sport, when Grace passed the Grubbs' dog Molly, a strange Dalmatian cross and no lightweight, across to rescuers.

Harry pushed Sport off him, and stepped around the crowd who'd emptied the sack—Grace's T-shirt—of puppies onto the bridge and were now oohing and aahing over them.

He was at the railing, reaching out for her, when the timbers groaned and shrieked, then something gave way and the little room was sucked beneath the water and the bridge.

'Grace!'

He saw her body flying through the air, registered a rope, and stood up on the railing, ready to dive in.

Paul stopped him.

'We slipped the loop of a lasso over her before she started passing the kids and dogs. She jumped clear as the timber gave way, so we'll just wait until she surfaces then haul her in.'

Haul her in?

As if she were a bag of sugar-cane mulch?

More anger, this time joining with the crippling concern he was feeling as he and all the watchers on the bridge searched the waters for a sight of her.

He grabbed the rope from the volunteer who was holding it and began to pull, feeling the dragging weight on the end of it, wondering if he was drowning Grace by pulling on it but needing to get her out of the water.

Others joined him, then her body, limply unconscious, surfaced by the bridge. Eager hands reached out to grab her, but as she was lifted from the water, Harry grasped her in his arms, vaguely hearing one of the paramedics giving orders, telling him to put her down, turn her on her side, check her pulse, her breathing.

But this was Grace and he hugged her to him,

although he knew he had to do as the man had said—had to put her down to save her life.

He dropped to his knees and gently laid her on the tarred surface of the road, seeing sharp gravel from the recent resurfacing—little stones that would dig into her skin.

That's when he knew, with gut-wrenching certainty, that it wasn't physical attraction—right then when he was thinking about sharp gravel pressing into Grace's skin…

CHAPTER TEN

THE two paramedics took over, moving him aside with kind firm hands, clearing her airway, forcing air into her lungs, breathing for her, then waiting, then breathing again.

No chest compressions, which meant her heart was beating, but somehow registering this information failed to make Harry feel any better.

He loved her?

The concept was so mind-blowing he had to keep repeating it to himself in the hope the three words would eventually become a statement, not an incredulous question.

Was it too late?

He watched the two men work, saw oxygen delivered through bag pressure and a needle being inserted into the back of her hand. But mostly he just watched her face, the skin so pale it took on a bluish hue, her freckles dark against it.

One day he'd kiss each freckle, and with each kiss repeat, 'I love you.' He'd make up for all the time they'd lost, he'd—

Sport abandoned his paramour and puppies and came to press against him. Harry dug his fingers into the dog's rough coat, despair crowding his senses as he looked into the animal's liquid brown eyes and made silent promises he hoped he'd have the opportunity to keep.

'We're moving her now,' one of the paramedics said, and together they lifted Grace onto a stretcher, raised it to wheeling height, then ran with it towards their ambulance.

Running? Did running mean the situation was even more disastrous than he imagined?

Harry followed at a jog, cursing himself now that he'd sat communing with his dog, now loping unsteadily beside him, when he should have been asking questions about Grace's condition.

'What do you think?' he demanded, arriving at the ambulance as the driver was shutting the back door.

'She's breathing on her own—although we're still assisting her—and her heart rate's OK, but she's unconscious so obviously she hit her head somewhere underwater. There'll be water in her lungs, and she'll have swallowed it as well, so all we can do is get her into hospital and pump antibiotics into her and hope the concussion resolves itself.'

Totally unsatisfactory, especially that last bit, Harry thought as he drove to the hospital behind the ambulance. His radio was chattering non-stop and he really should return to the meeting, but he had to see Grace first—wanted her conscious—wanted to tell her…

But seeing Grace was one thing—speaking to her impossible.

'You're needed other places, Harry. I'll contact you if there's any change at all.'

Harry wanted to shrug off the hand Charles was resting on his arm and tell the man to go to hell, but he knew Charles was right. There was nothing he could do here, except glare at the nursing staff and grunt when the doctors told him all they could do was wait and see.

Wait and see what, for heaven's sake?

Frustration grumbled within him, and tiredness, so heavy he could barely keep upright, blurred his senses. He left the hospital, pausing in the car park to call the station and tell them he was going home to sleep for an hour then back to the civic centre to hear the latest in the evacuation and services restoration plans.

Power had to come first—without it water and sewerage systems failed to work. It would be reconnected first in the area this side of the creek, the original settlement, where the hospital and police station were. But with the flooding…

On top of that, there was still no word from Georgie—not since the one radio transmission that might or might not have come from her. She had his radio—why *hadn't* she called in?

It was the inactivity on that front that ate at him. Until the road was cleared they couldn't get vehicles in, while the heavy rain made an air search impossible. It was still too wet and windy for one of the light helicopters to fly searchers in—if they had searchers available.

Which they didn't! Sending sleep-depleted volunteers into the mountains was asking for trouble.

So all he could do was wait. Wait for the army, with its fresh and experienced manpower, and heavy-duty helicopters that could cope with wind and rain.

Or wait to hear.

And keep believing that she and Alistair were sensible people and would stay safe...

At midnight, when exhausted city officials and the first wave of army brass had headed for whatever beds they could find, Harry returned to the hospital. Grace, he was told, was in the ICU.

'Intensive Care? What's she doing in there?' he demanded, and a bemused nurse who'd probably only ever seen nice-guy Harry, looked startled.

'She's unconscious and running a low-grade fever and has fluid in her lungs so it's likely she's hatching pneumonia, in which case the fever could get worse. And on top of that there's the chance it's something nastier than pneumonia. Who knows what germs were lurking in that water?'

And having set him back on his heels, almost literally, with this information, the nurse gave a concerned smile.

'We're *all* very worried about her, Harry,' she added, just in case he thought he was the only one concerned.

Harry nodded, and even tried to smile, but that was too damn difficult when Grace was lying in Intensive Care, incubating who knew what disease.

He strode towards the isolated unit, determined to see her, but no one blocked his path or muttered about family only.

She was lying in the bed, beneath a sheet, wires and tubes snaking from her body.

So small and fragile-looking—still as death.

Gina sat beside her, holding her hand and talking to her. She looked up at Harry and, although wobbly, at least *her* smile was working.

'She always talks to coma patients when she's nursing them,' Gina said, her eyes bright with unshed tears. 'I thought it was the least I could do.'

Then the tears spilled over and slipped down her cheeks.

'She saved my son. She plunged into that filthy, stinking water and swam out to save him. She can't die, Harry, she just can't.'

'She won't,' Harry promised, although he knew it was a promise he couldn't make come true. Gina stood up and he slipped into the chair and took the warm, pale hand she passed to him.

Grace's hand, so small and slight, Grace's fingers, nails neatly trimmed.

'Does she know?' Gina asked, and Harry, puzzled by the question, turned towards her. 'That you love her?' Gina expanded, with a much better smile this time.

'No,' he said, the word cutting deep inside his chest as he thought of Grace dying without knowing. Then he, too, smiled. 'But I'm here to tell her and I'll keep on telling her. You're right, she does believe unconscious patients hear things, so surely she'll be listening.'

He paused, then said awkwardly to Gina, 'She loves me, you know. She told me earlier today.'

It must have been the wonder in his voice that made Gina chuckle. She leant forward and hugged him.

'That's not exactly news, you know, Harry. The entire hospital's known how Grace felt for the past six months.'

'She told you?' Harry muttered. 'Told everyone but me?'

Gina smiled again, a kindly smile.

'Would you have listened?' she said softly, then she gave him another hug. 'And she didn't tell us all in words, you know. We just saw it in the way she lit up whenever you were around and the way she said your name and the way she glowed on meeting nights. There are a thousand ways to say "I love you", Harry, and I think your Grace knows most of them.'

'*My* Grace,' Harry muttered, unable to believe he hadn't seen what everyone else had. Hadn't seen the thousand ways Grace had said 'I love you'. But Gina was already gone, pausing in the doorway to tell him Cal would be by later and to promise that Grace would have someone sitting with her all the time, talking to her and holding her hand so she could find her way back from wherever she was right now.

Again it was Charles who told Harry to leave.

'I don't ever sleep late—growing up on a cattle property in the tropics, where the best work was done before the heat of midday, instils the habit of early waking.'

He'd wheeled into the room while Harry had been dozing in the chair, his body bent forward so his head rested on Grace's bed, her hand still clasped in his.

'So I'm doing the early shift with Grace,' Charles continued, manoeuvring his chair into position. 'If you want some technicalities, her breathing and pulse rate suggest she's regaining consciousness but the infection's taking hold and her temperature is fluctuating rather alarmingly.'

Harry knew he had to go. He had to get some sleep then return to the planning room. Evacuation of people who had family or friends to go to close by had begun yesterday and today they were hoping to begin mass evacuation of up to a thousand women and children. Defence force transport planes would bring in water, tents, food and building supplies and fly people out to Townsville or Cairns. Power would come on in stages, and it could be months before all services were fully operational. Getting people out of the crippled town would ease the pressure on the limited services.

He left the hospital reluctantly, and was in a meeting when Cal phoned to say Grace had regained consciousness but was feverish and disoriented, mostly sleeping, which was good.

Harry raged against the constraints that held him in the meeting, knowing he couldn't go rushing to Grace's side when he was needed right where he was. But later…

Later she was sleeping, so he slipped into the chair vacated this time for him by her friend Marcia, and took her hand, talking quietly to her, telling her he was there.

Grace turned her head and opened her eyes, gazing at him with a puzzled frown. Then the frown cleared, as if she'd worked out who he was, and she said, 'Go away Harry,' as clear as day.

Nothing else, just, 'Go away Harry.' Then she shut her eyes again as if not seeing him would make him vanish.

She was feverish, he told himself, and didn't know what she was saying, but when she woke an hour later and saw him there, her eyes filled with tears and this time the knife she used to stab right into his heart was phrased differently.

'I don't want you here, Harry,' she said, her voice piteously weak, the single tear sliding down her cheek doing further damage to his already lacerated heart.

Cal was there, and his quiet 'I don't want her getting upset' got Harry to his feet.

But go?

How could he walk away and leave her lying there, so still and pale beneath the sheet?

'There's work for you to do elsewhere,' Cal reminded him, following him out of the ICU and stopping beside the wide window where Cal had propped himself. 'I'll keep you posted about her condition.'

So Harry worked and listened to Cal telling him Grace was as well as could be expected, not exactly improving but the new antibiotics they were trying seemed to be keeping the infection stable.

It was in her lungs and now he had to worry if pulling her through the water had made things worse, but there were no answers to that kind of question so he worked some more, and went home to sleep from time to time, to feed Sport and talk to him of love.

On the third day after Willie had blown the town apart, Grace was moved out of the ICU and two days later released from hospital, but only as far as the doctors' house, where resident medical staff could fuss over her and keep an eye on her continuing improvement at the same time.

So it was there that Harry went, late one afternoon, when the urgency had left the restoration programme and he could take time off without feeling guilty.

She was on the veranda, Gina told him. On the old couch. As he walked through the house he sensed Gina tactfully making sure all the other residents had vamoosed.

He came out onto the veranda and there was Grace, pale but pretty, her golden curls shining in the sun that had finally blessed them with its presence and what looked like a dirty black rag draped across her knees.

'Grace?' he said, hating the fact he sounded so tentative, yet fearful she'd once again send him away.

'Harry?'

The word echoed with surprise, as if he was the last person she expected to be calling on her.

A thought that added to his tension!

'Come and sit down. I'm not supposed to move about much. One lung collapsed during all the fuss and it's not quite better yet, so I'm stuck in bed or on the couch, but at least from here I can see the sea. It's quietened down a lot, hasn't it?'

Harry stared at her. This was the Grace he used to know. Actually, it was a much frailer and quieter and less bubbly version of her, but still that Grace, the one who was his friend. Chatting to him, easing over difficult moments—showing love?

He had no idea—totally confused by what he'd come

to realise after that terrible moment when Grace had disappeared beneath the murky floodwaters and then by the 'go away' order she'd issued from the hospital bed.

Stepping tentatively, although the old house had withstood Willie's fury better than most of the houses in town, he moved towards the couch, then sat where Grace was patting the space beside her on the couch.

'I thought I'd lost you,' he began, then wondered if she was well enough for him to be dumping his emotions on her. 'You disappeared beneath the waters and I realised what a fool I'd been, Grace. Stupid, stupid fool, hiding away from any emotion all this time, letting the mess I'd made of my marriage to Nikki overshadow my life, then, worst of all, blaming physical attraction for the kiss. I know it's too late to be telling you all this—that somehow with the bump on your head you got some common sense and decided you could do far better than me—but, like you had to say it when I thought I'd lost Sport, so I have to say it now. I love you, Grace.'

Having bumbled his way this far through the conversation, Harry paused and looked at the recipient of all this information. She was staring at him as if he'd spoken in tongues, so he tried again.

'I love you, Grace,' he said, and wondered if he should perhaps propose right now and make a total fool of himself all at once, or leave the foolish proposal part for some other time.

'You love me?' she finally whispered, and he waited for the punch-line, the 'Oh, Harry, it's too late' or however she might word it.

But nothing followed so he took her hands in his and nodded, then as tension gripped so hard it hurt, he rushed into speech again.

'I know you don't feel the same way but you did love me once, so maybe that love is only hidden, not completely gone.'

'Loved you once?' she said, and this time the repetition was stronger, and now her blue eyes were fixed on his. 'What makes you think I'd ever stop loving you, Harry?'

He stared at her, trying to work out what this question meant—trying to equate it with the 'go away, Harry' scenarios.

Couldn't do it, so he had to ask.

'You sent me away,' he reminded her. 'At the hospital, you said to go away and that you didn't want me there.'

'Oh, Harry,' she whispered, and rested her head against his chest. 'You silly man, thinking I'd stopped loving you. As soon stop the sun from rising as me stop loving you.'

This definitely made him happy, happy enough to press a kiss to her soft curls, but he was still confused. Maybe more confused than ever.

'But you sent me away when all I wanted was to be with you.'

She turned towards him and lifted one hand to rest it on his cheek.

'I didn't want you sitting by my bedside—not at that hospital—not again. I didn't want you remembering all that pain and anguish, and suffering for things that happened in the past through no real fault of yours.'

She pressed her lips to his, a present of a kiss.

'The fact that you talked about Nikki and your marriage suggested you were ready to move on, so I didn't want you being pulled back into the past because of me.'

'You'd have liked me there?' Harry asked, unable to believe that, sick as she had been, she'd still found this one way of the thousand to say 'I love you'.

'Of course,' she whispered, nestling her head on his chest. 'Loving you the way I do, I always want you near.'

She smiled up at him, then added, 'Look how pathetic I am—look at this.'

She lifted the black rag from her knee and it took a moment for him to recognise it as his dinner jacket.

'I brushed off most of the mud and when Gina said I had to keep something over my knees when I sit out in the breeze, it seemed the best knee cover any woman could have. Gina wanted to have it dry-cleaned but it would have come back smelling of dry-cleaning fluid, not Harry, so there you are.'

Her smile mocked her sentimentality but it went straight to Harry's heart, because it wobbled a bit as if she felt she'd made a fool of herself.

'Snap!' he said softly, and reached into his shirt pocket, pulling out a very tattered blue ribbon he'd kept with him since that fateful night.

Then he closed his arms around her and pulled her close, pressing kisses on her head and telling her things he hadn't realised he knew, about how much he loved her, but more, that he admired her and thought her wonderful, and how soon would she be his wife?

They'd reached the kissing stage when a voice interrupted them, a voice filled with the disgust that only a five-year-old could muster when faced with demonstrations of love.

'You're kissing, Grace,' CJ said, coming close enough for them to see he held a squirming puppy in his hands. 'I didn't think policemen did that kind of thing.'

'Well, now you know they do,' Harry said, tucking Grace tightly against his body, never wanting to let her go.

CJ sighed.

'Then I guess I'll have to be a fireman instead,' he said, passing the puppy to Harry. 'Mum said you were here, and this is the one Lily and I decided should be yours because it looks more like Sport than all the others, although it's got four legs.'

Harry took the squirming bundle of fur and peered into its face. He failed to see any resemblance at all to Sport, but knew once CJ and Lily had decided something, it was futile to argue.

'Do you mind if we have two dogs?' he asked Grace, who smiled at him so lovingly he had to kiss her again, further disgusting CJ, who rescued the pup and departed, making fire-siren noises as he raced away.

'Two dogs and lots of kids,' Grace said, returning his kisses with enthusiasm. 'Is that OK with you?'

Harry thought of all he now knew about Grace's

background. Loving without being loved must have been so hard for someone with her warm and caring nature.

'Of course we'll have lots of kids,' he promised, and was about to suggest they start on the project right now when he remembered she was just out of hospital and very frail.

But not too frail to kiss him as she whispered, 'Thank you.' Then added, 'I love you, Harry Blake,' and made his day complete.

MILLS & BOON®
MEDICAL™
Proudly presents

Brides of Penhally Bay

Featuring Dr Nick Tremayne

*A pulse-raising collection of emotional, tempting romances and
heart-warming stories – devoted doctors, single fathers,
Mediterranean heroes, a Sheikh and his guarded heart,
royal scandals and miracle babies…*

Book One
CHRISTMAS EVE BABY
by Caroline Anderson

Starting 7th December 2007

MILLS & BOON®

MEDICAL™

Proudly presents

Brides of Penhally Bay

A pulse-raising collection of emotional, tempting romances and heart-warming stories by bestselling Mills & Boon Medical™ authors.

January 2008
The Italian's New-Year Marriage Wish
by **Sarah Morgan**

Enjoy some much-needed winter warmth with gorgeous Italian doctor Marcus Avanti.

February 2008
The Doctor's Bride By Sunrise
by **Josie Metcalfe**

Then join Adam and Maggie on a 24-hour rescue mission where romance begins to blossom as the sun starts to set.

March 2008
The Surgeon's Fatherhood Surprise
by **Jennifer Taylor**

Single dad Jack Tremayne finds a mother for his little boy – and a bride for himself.

Let us whisk you away to an idyllic Cornish town – a place where hearts are made whole

COLLECT ALL 12 BOOKS!

4 FREE

BOOKS AND A SURPRISE GIFT!

We would like to take this opportunity to thank you for reading this Mills & Boon® book by offering you the chance to take FOUR more specially selected titles from the Medical™ series absolutely FREE! We're also making this offer to introduce you to the benefits of the Mills & Boon® Reader Service™—

- ★ **FREE home delivery**
- ★ **FREE gifts and competitions**
- ★ **FREE monthly Newsletter**
- ★ **Exclusive Reader Service offers**
- ★ **Books available before they're in the shops**

Accepting these FREE books and gift places you under no obligation to buy, you may cancel at any time, even after receiving your free shipment. Simply complete your details below and return the entire page to the address below. You don't even need a stamp!

YES! Please send me 4 free Medical books and a surprise gift. I understand that unless you hear from me, I will receive 6 superb new titles every month for just £2.89 each, postage and packing free. I am under no obligation to purchase any books and may cancel my subscription at any time. The free books and gift will be mine to keep in any case.

M7ZED

Ms/Mrs/Miss/Mr ....Initials ....
BLOCK CAPITALS PLEASE

Surname ....

Address ....

....

....Postcode.............................

Send this whole page to:
UK: FREEPOST CN81, Croydon, CR9 3WZ